A Strange Band On An Even Stranger Quest

There was M'Cord, the loner, an Earthling adventurer who did not fear to go where no human had ever trod before on the great wastelands of Mars. There was Thaklar, heir to the lost greatness of the planet, and possessor of its most sacred secret. There was Zerild, the Martian dancing girl who was mistress of the art of sensual enslavement, and Chastar, the murderous outlaw in her power. There was the corrupt spoiled priest Phuun, as cunning as he was evil, and the lost and terrified sibling scientists from Earth, Inga and Karl Nordgren.

Each of them was possessed by a fevered desire to discover the fabled lost Eden of Mars, the home of the ancient gods, from which no living creature had ever returned—and where they would find either unimaginable power or hideous doom. . . .

THE VALLEY
WHERE TIME STOOD STILL

BY LIN CARTER
THE VALLEY WHERE TIME STOOD STILL

WILDSIDE PRESS

www.wildsidepress.com

*All the characters in this book are ficti-
tious, and any resemblance to actual persons, living or dead is purely coincidental.*

For Leigh Brackett
because it's her kind of story.

Three Extracts

He maketh me to lie down in green pastures: he leadeth me beside the still waters. He restoreth my soul: he leadeth me in the paths of righteousness for his name's sake. Yea, though I walk through the valley of the shadow of death, I will fear no evil.

The Bible/King James version/Philadelphia, 1947.

None cometh from thence that he may tell thee how they fare, that he may tell thee of their fortunes, that he may comfort our hearts, until we also depart to the place whither they have gone. O, no man returneth again who is gone thither.

The Book of the Dead/Wallis Budge version/London, 1923.

There is a land where no man ventures; for no man cometh back therefrom once he hath entered in. But even in the Valley of Life he that is pure of heart need not fear; even in the Valley Where Life Was Born the pure have naught to fear. But woe unto him who is not pure of heart; for therein shall be given to each according to his deserving.

The Book/Martinez-Schuster translation/Syrtis, 2031.

I

THE WAY
TO
YGNARH

I. Just This Side of Death

Vultures gather at the scent of death and circle lazily on the wind. You can see them for miles, far up, black flecks against the acetylene-blue, and when you see them, you know that death came by this place today.

There are no vultures on Mars; the air is too thin for birds of any kind. But *slidars* can smell death on the dry, cold air as well as any Earthside scavenger.

The natives break and tame *slidars* for riding-beasts. But in the wild, the ungainly, long-legged scarlet reptiles are carrion eaters, and they love the smell of dead things on the desert air.

The *slidar* M'Cord was riding jerked its head up at the scent of death. Ignoring the bite of the mouth rings as the reins pulled taut, it twisted its head about, flexing its long, snaky neck. Fanged jaws agape, it hissed hungrily at the taste in the air.

M'Cord had been prospecting the equatorial dustlands for ten years and he knew the way of *slidars* well. The beast sidled, tossing its head restlessly, uttering the wailing cry of its kind.

He knew what the *slidar* knew.

Something nearby was dead; or dying.

He gave the brute its head, loosening the reins. The ungainly reptile broke into its loose-jointed, loping stride. *Slidar* means "loper" in the Tongue. The beasts are aptly named; they shamble with the splay-footed stride of camels.

It was just past midday. The sun burned bright but gave no warmth, cold against the cold dusky sky that was bruise-purple rather than blue, for the air was thinner here than on Earth. M'Cord had left the colony of Sun Lake City three months ago; he had taken a wandering, circuitous route through Tharsis and Xanthe and across the Hydraotes into the dustlands of Southern Chryse. He was heading for the uplands of Eos to do some scouting around the canyons along the coast of Mare Erythraeum.

But he was in no particular hurry to get there.

He was a hard-faced, lanky Earthsider, lean and rangy, with long legs and cold gray eyes. His people had been of the Black Irish from County Kerry, but somewhere along the line a dour, dry strain of Highlands Scots had entered his blood. He was shrewd and tough and a mean man with a knife in a barroom brawl. He had been hurt, once, long ago, and never got over it. Now he hurt back, whenever he could; but mostly he kept to himself, closemouthed and hard-eyed, a man with few acquaintances and no friends.

Only a Low Clan woman with black silk hair and little crystal bells woven in it, who kept a room for him on a back alley in Sun Lake behind the Presidium, knew that he could be tender at times, and could laugh when he wanted to.

But she knew, too, that when the black mood was on him he could be harsh and even cruel.

He was cruelest of all to himself; that was M'Cord's way.

He let his loper follow the smell of death that rode on the bitter air. This was the Aram Desert, smack on the

12

equator at about eleven degrees west longitude. No one lived here; there was not even a camping-place of the People within a thousand miles, and the nearest Earthsider colony was Sun Lake.

No one lived here because here nothing could survive. The yellow dustland was like talcum, desiccated and sterile. Even the rare predators who lived in the desert countries avoided Aram.

M'Cord wondered, then, what it was that had died.

Sometimes a skimmer comes down in the dustlands, its flimsy airfoils punctured by micrometeorites. It might be a colonist; it might even be a CA cop.

M'Cord grinned at the thought, a hard grin that pulled his lean cheeks taut and bared his teeth. A grin like a fighting snarl.

He had no love for cops.

But it wasn't a CA patrol skimmer, it was a dead loper. With a man pinned under it, not dead, but not far from it, either.

He was a native, M'Cord knew, from his coppery-red skin and russet furcap. A big man, strong, with long arms and long legs corded with tough sinew, and a lean harsh face, grim and expressionless. A face of dry, burned leather in which only his yellow eyes lived and moved.

He lay on his back, propped up on his left elbow, and he watched M'Cord come up to him without a word or a gesture.

His left leg was pinned under the dead beast.

His right leg was drawn up flat against the loper's big shoulder. He had been trying to push the corpse off him, using only his foot. He had been trying to do that for three days and nights.

His lips were dry and cracked. His tongue was black

13

and swollen. The flesh on his face and neck had fallen in and hard bone and lean sinew stood out in sharp relief.

Beside him on the powdery sand lay a flat waterskin. It was long-since dry, and he had ripped it open, reversed it, and chewed the lining to suck up the last trace of moisture.

He was just this side of death; but he was still fighting.

His right hand lay on his thigh. It clasped an energy gun.

The gun was not lifted, pointing at M'Cord; but it was out and ready.

He lay there, unspeaking, watching the Earthsider with yellow, hating eyes.

M'Cord pulled up and sat in the saddle, looking at the Martian and thinking it out.

Neither said a word.

The natives hate Earthsider colonists; but they hate CA cops even more. M'Cord was neither, but it made no difference. For more than half a century M'Cord's fellow countrymen had looted and bilked and robbed the last remnants of a proud and ancient race of warriors. Plundered their tombs and holy places, raped their women, and chained the men to slave in the barium mines.

To the People, all Earthsiders are the *F'yagha*—the Hated Ones. And M'Cord was a *F'yagh*.

But they who roam the dustlands share a common code. Survival in the hostile, powdery deserts is infinitely difficult. Here, a man helps another in need, and blood-feud and clan-war alike are of no importance.

M'Cord slid out of the saddle, but slowly, keeping both hands clearly in sight. He came around the dead *slidar* toward the helpless man. The native lay motionless, watching him come without a word; but his fingers tightened on the butt of his energy weapon.

Belted low on his lean hips, M'Cord wore two guns of his own, of course. No one rides out of the Wetlands

14

without a weapon by his side. There is no law beyond Tharsis. So M'Cord packed two power pistols; they were old and worn, but General Electric had built them to last. M'Cord could have them unholstered and ready for action in a tenth of a second.

Before he came up to the prone figure pinned under the dead *slidar*, M'Cord stopped, slowly and carefully unbuckled his gunbelt, and let it fall in the dust behind him.

The native's yellow eyes watched him, hard and cold and fierce as a hawk, as he knelt by his side and unsnapped one of the two canteens he wore.

"This water is not my property," M'Cord said slowly and as clearly as he could, wishing he knew the Tongue better than he did. "I found it in the desert. It belongs to no one. I will leave it here for anyone who passes."

Then he sat back, squatting on his heels, watching as the half-dead native picked up the full canteen in trembling hands, unscrewed the cap, and drank.

He did not offer to help, although the man was feeble and far gone. Neither did he address him directly. To the Martians, water is a precious thing, and a sacred. The sharing of water is a ritual that means much to them. One does not casually offer a drink, for the acceptance of water from the hands of another establishes a bond of rare intimacy, like blood-brotherhood; and one neither offers nor accepts such a bond lightly.

But in denying ownership of the canteen, M'Cord made it possible for the clansman to take it without obligation.

He watched as the man drank. First he only moistened his lips; then he wet his tongue; finally, he took a cautious sip into his mouth and held it there for a time before painfully swallowing.

To survive in the dustlands you must learn how to use water. After three days' exposure, had the native drunk deeply, as he yearned to drink, it could have killed him.

His tissues, by now, were dehydrated; a bellyful of cold water could have sent him into convulsions.

The man took another shallow sip, cherished it, swallowed slowly. Then, although his fingers trembled with yearning, he refastened the screw seal and set the canteen beside him. He would repeat these actions in thirty minutes or so, M'Cord knew.

He studied the man thoughtfully, with narrowed eyes. This was no rider of the Low Clans, surely, but a warrior princeling of the High Blood, from his fine bones and keen eyes and lean, aristocratic symmetry. Low-clansmen are coarser of feature and wear their furcaps trimmed in a different fashion.

This man was very far from home.

M'Cord wondered why he had come to this place.

And where he was going.

The *slidar* had not suffered an injury, or none that M'Cord could see. But he was surely dead, and had been dead for days. Had this been Earth, and the beast a horse instead of a loper, the warrior could have cut a vein and drunk the beast's blood. But there is a substance in the blood of *slidars* that reacts with some enzyme in a Martian's system and makes a poison. Thus the warrior had been dying a slow death from thirst, and would soon have perished had not M'Cord decided to give his steed its head and see what it had scented on the dry air.

He tended the native as best he could. First he dragged aside the corpse, freeing the Martian's leg. It was broken below the knee, a clean break, as far as he could tell. He splinted the femur with two plastron rods kept in his medikit against just such need, and bound the leg tightly with celluflex.

The warrior lay and watched him without a word. He grunted once as M'Cord set the bone, but that was all.

16

When it was over he wet his lips from the canteen again and took another mouthful of water. M'Cord gave him a ration of beef stew in one of those self-heating containers. The warrior wolfed it down hungrily, never noticing the pain-killer and full set of antibiotics M'Cord had slipped in when his back had been turned.

When at last the clansman decided to speak, it was gruffly, and in a harsh, croaking voice.

"Are you a 'god-peddler,' *F'yagh?*" he rasped, meaning a missionary.

M'Cord shook his head. "Your gods are your own," he said, "and mine are mine." He knew how the People felt toward missionaries; they have little love for such, and speak of them with dry contempt.

The warrior grunted.

"I was near my gods this day," he said grimly, with a little laugh. "So close was I to the Bridge of Fire, I could feel the heat of the flames against my feet!"

M'Cord nodded somberly. "Yhoom was not yet ready to welcome your spirit," he said, for he had read The Book once or twice. "Mayhap the Timeless Ones have yet a task for you here."

The Martian eyed him without curiosity.

"My name is Thaklar," he said grudgingly. But he did not name his clan, M'Cord noticed.

He gave him his name; the Martian wrinkled his face at the sound of it.

". . . 'Gort?" he said, not finding it easy to pronounce.

"Close enough," shrugged M'Cord. "Do you have the strength to ride?"

They made ten miles before sunfall, Thaklar swaying, bent in the saddle, dozing, with M'Cord trudging on foot through the powdery yellow sand, leading the *slidar* by the reins.

When the sun died and the stars flamed forth, bright as ice-blue diamonds in a sky like black velvet, they had

17

reached the Oxus and camped for the night on the rubbery blue moss. M'Cord carried only one thermosac in his saddlebags, so they slept together. But they were not yet friends, the Earthsider and the Martian . . . who was three thousand miles from where he ought to be.

II. Dragon Hawk

M'Cord was up getting water before dawn. The Oxus is one of thirty-four thousand such strips of rudimentary vegetation that crisscross the surface of Mars and which Earthside astronomers of a couple of centuries ago mistakenly called canals.

Mars has been drying up for seventy-three million years. When a planet dries its crust cracks, and if it has a crust like that of Mars—mostly a combination of silicon and magnesium-salts—the crystalline stuff cracks with geometrical regularity. What water remained from the drying-up of the primeval oceans drained into these cracks, and the hardy Martian vegetation rooted there, making long strips of knee-high, rubbery-leafed mosses whose root systems extend over a mile beneath the surface.

The rubbery leaves are tougher than leather, but you can extract the moisture by using a pressure-still; which is how desert prospectors of M'Cord's breed can survive for many months without having to find an oasis every few days.

While his morning crop of fat, juicy leaves were perco-

19

lating in the still, M'Cord roved about, checking the ground with a hand indicator. His guest sprawled lazily on the deflated thermosac, watching him, puzzled. At last his curiosity got the better of his natural taciturnity.

"What is it that you do, 'Gort?"

"I search for 'power-metal,' Thaklar," answered M'Cord, meaning uranium. The warrior nodded thoughtfully: the *F'yagha*, he knew, had a strange lust for the crumbly gray ore, which he knew to be worthless. It was but one of the many mysteries about the Outworlders that baffled him.

He grunted. "And if you find metal, 'Gort?"

"If I find much metal, then I am a rich man, Thaklar," M'Cord said, truthfully enough.

The Martian laughed—a peculiar, snarling sound with contempt in it, and little humor. "Then you will fly to your home world in a sky machine, 'Gort!" he observed. "I hope that you find much metal. I would that all of the *F'yagha* in the world could find much metal; then they would all fly home in sky machines and leave us in peace."

"That would not happen, Thaklar," M'Cord said, grinning. "If very much power-metal were found, very many more of my people would come here, because every man wishes to become wealthy."

"*Aeiii!* Then I give thanks to the Timeless Ones that the world is poor in power-metal, and would that it were even poorer!" Thaklar moaned. It was as close to making a joke as he had yet come, and M'Cord smiled at him.

The warrior, however, did not return the smile. M'Cord had saved his life, and he knew it. But he was still a *F'yagh*—still a Hated One. Down deep inside, somewhere, Thaklar may have felt gratitude toward the Earthling; but not necessarily. The Martians were barbarians, having lost the high civilization they once had in the

20

Upper Cretaceous. Like all barbarians, they were savage, cruel, and thoroughly unpredictable.

Or so M'Cord believed, anyway. And he still turned his back on Thaklar with a certain degree of trepidation. The warrior was perfectly capable of shooting him in the back, if only to take his mount and his gear. They were not yet friends; but they were not exactly foes, either. A sort of armed truce stretched between them, and probably a temporary one at that.

"If you're strong enough to make jokes, you're strong enough to get breakfast started," M'Cord said, pointing toward the saddlebags. Thaklar gave him a yellowy glare but did not smile. After a while he got up, hobbling stiff-legged, and began to search through the bag.

They ate self-heated cans of scrambled eggs and bacon bits, and drank black coffee that had a metallic aftertaste, which was a lingering flavor from the processed water from the moss leaves. Fresh coffee was a mad luxury on Mars, but M'Cord insisted on it.

Then they rode on, with M'Cord still afoot, again leading the loper.

"Where is it that you go, 'Gort, in seeking the power-metal?" Thaklar asked about an hour later.

M'Cord shrugged. "Up toward Eos, and along the Erythraeum," he said, but he used the native terms rather than the Earthsider geographical names.

Thaklar meditated on that. After a while M'Cord dared to ask where *he* had been heading when his beast died. It was a bit risky, that question. It was strictly against Custom to inquire into the personal business of a newly met acquaintance. He was not particularly surprised that Thaklar pointedly kept silent. The silence continued for half an hour more. Then, unexpectedly, the warrior spoke up.

"I go south and east," he said flatly.

"Then we are going in opposite directions," M'Cord remarked.

Thaklar said nothing.

M'Cord plodded along, not caring for conversation anyway. His thighs ached and the muscles in the backs of his legs were on fire from the unusual exercise of trudging through ankle-deep powdery sand.

"There is no power-metal in the high country," said Thaklar, unexpectedly breaking silence again.

"Maybe not; but that's where I'm going," M'Cord grunted, too tired to bother being diplomatic.

Another interval of silence; this time it lasted for about twenty minutes.

"If you were going south and east, I could show you power-metal," Thaklar said.

M'Cord stopped and bent over to massage his weary calves. While he did so, he thought about it. Thaklar still wore his energy weapon; he was perfectly capable of drawing it, forcing M'Cord to disarm, and making him head southeast at gunpoint. Or, M'Cord grimly reminded himself, of shooting him down where he stood, and going on alone. This sort of slow-motion effort at persuasion was, quite obviously, a gesture of something like friendship.

South and east. That sounded like Deucalionis Regio, or the Sabaeus Sinus Plateau. What in the world did Thaklar hope to find in that part of the country? The plateau was a dead wilderness of sterile rock, cleft asunder by a thousand canyons and ravines; Deucalionis was a curved tongue of dustland that extended into the highlands between two plateaux. Seventy million years ago it had been a bay, perhaps, or a river delta, cut deep into a continental coast. Now it was nothing: dead rock, scoured with sand, where few wild beasts roamed.

The trouble was, M'Cord wasn't going there. He had his heart set on the coastal canyons of the big Mare to the west.

22

And he was damn well going where *he* wanted to!

Instead of saying no, he temporized by chancing another question.

"Are you bound for a camp of your people?"

This time, for some reason, the answer came swiftly.

"My people are my business, *F'yagh*."

"Didn't mean to pry. Sorry."

"I . . . have no people. I am *aoudh*," Thaklar said heavily, using an untranslatable term whose meaning lay somewhere between "outlaw" and "orphan," or at least, "one who has no kin."

" 'The gods are father to every man,' " M'Cord quoted.

Again, the interval of silence.

Then grudgingly: "An Outworlder that knows The Book? You are certain, 'Gort, you are no god-peddler?"

M'Cord was too weary to smile. "I've been here for ten years. I learned the Tongue. Often I live and work among your people—"

Stung, Thaklar stiffened in the saddle. "Not among *my* people!"

M'Cord made an offhand gesture. "The Low Clans, I mean."

"I am a warrior of the High Blood, Outworlder!"

"I know you are. Must we quarrel? I am weary."

Thaklar bent a fierce yellow gaze on him as he stumbled along painfully, slump-shouldered. When he spoke, it was in a softer tone.

"I ride in comfort, while you tread the dust like a slave. Why is this?"

M'Cord felt like hitting him. "I walk because I must, damn you! You ride because you have a broken leg."

Pride flamed in the hawk face of the Martian.

He jerked back on the reins, bringing the scarlet beast to a sudden halt. Painfully, he swung one leg up over the saddlebow.

"I can walk. *You* will ride."

23

"Get back up there, you damned fool!" M'Cord swore, starting forward. Suddenly he was looking down the muzzle of an energy gun. He stopped short, glaring first at the gun, then at Thaklar's obstinate face.

"I am a Dragon Hawk warrior; no *F'yagh* from the Wetlands does me favor! Get into the saddle, 'Gort; I will lead the beast."

"You can't walk five steps, and you know it. So stop acting like a woman," M'Cord growled.

The Martian hissed and spat. His furcap ruffled like hackles.

"You . . . call me . . . *woman?*"

M'Cord matched him glare for glare.

"I call you a damn fool. Get back up in that saddle! I do you no favor, Thaklar. I walk because I know that you cannot. Are these not the dustlands? Is it not Custom for one man to help another here?"

The pistol did not waver. M'Cord looked down the cold black eye of the muzzle, breathing heavily.

"Go on, shoot me down, then. Is it thus the Dragon Hawk warriors treat men who have done them no hurt? Shoot me down—and take *all* the water!"

It was cleverly said. To accuse a man of acting from water-motive was to strike at the roots of his honor. It was not so much an insult as a crushing stroke of ultimate contempt.

Silence stretched tight, almost to the snapping point. Sweat trickled down M'Cord's ribs under his thermalsuit. The back of his mouth was dry, but he held his face rigid and impassive as iron, fearing to swallow and seem afraid.

Something almost like admiration gleamed briefly and was gone in the fierce yellow eyes of the other. He holstered the gun and attempted to remount the saddle, but could not, because of the leg, so M'Cord gave him a hoist.

Neither man had anything to say, but now the silence between them was somehow comfortable and without strain.

An hour past noon, they rested.

M'Cord was heading for Oxia Palus. There, at the junction of five minor canals, was a commo station. It was untended, of course, only an emergency radio beacon, but M'Cord knew he could put a call through to Mareotis, where the People kept a sort of embassy and where the Colonial Administration maintained a combination trading post and first aid station. A medic in a skimmer could be there in two days, three at the most, with one of the native *Hndolanthi*. A *Hndolanth* is a kind of interpreter-cum-herald. He said as much to Thaklar.

Again, the customary interval of grim silence between morsels of conversation. M'Cord was getting heartily sick of it.

Then Thaklar opened the breast of the fur-lined leather shirt he wore. When he laid his breast bare M'Cord saw the Dragon Hawk emblem tattooed about his heart.

From an inner pocket Thaklar withdrew a small round object.

"If you will take me south and east, into Chumndar Draw, I will give you—*this.*"

He held out his hand and opened it. He was holding a *ziriol* the size of a small walnut.

M'Cord said nothing, but his eyes widened.

A *ziriol* is a purple ruby, a kind found only on Mars. Prized among Earthside jewelers, the gems are immensely, even fabulously, rare. A ruby that size—and it looked to be of the finest water—was worth something in the neighborhood of five hundred thousand dollars.

Even in CA scrip, that's a lot of dollars.

In ten years of bumming around the dustlands—a little smuggling here, a bit of gun-running there, and quite a lot of prospecting everywhere—M'Cord had yet to garner a tenth of the sum.

25

He reached out, picked it up, examined it closely. No counterfeit; the gem was true. And superb. A taint of vanadium salts in the ruby matrix produced the rare, imperial purple shade.

The gem he held cupped in his palm could set him up for life. Oh, maybe not with a villa on the Riviera and a bungalow on the fashionable South Slope of Everest and a hunting cabin in the Antarctica Game Preserve, but he could live comfortably enough for all his years on what that gem would bring in the side streets of Amsterdam.

He tossed the shimmering crystal back to Thaklar, who snatched it deftly from the air. Then he dug out his battered compass, took a squint at the sun, and gestured off to one side.

"Chumndar Draw is over that way, I think. We'd better get started."

III. Fear Has Yellow Eyes

It was hard going, but they took it easy, frequently stopping to rest. Since M'Cord had to slog along on foot, these rest stops were imperative. He was a big man, and strong, and as tough as they come, but wading through ankle-deep powdery sand was as hard as wading through viscous mud, and one tires easily on Mars. That's because of the air, which is thin and cold and so dry that it makes a wintry day on the Andean Plateau seem like the humid depths of the Matto Grosso.

The gravity was no problem—at an apparent fraction of his Earthside weight, M'Cord was as spry and nimble as a boy. No, it was the air—cold enough to sear your throat lining and dry enough to burn your lungs, and starved for oxygen. Long ago it had been commonly accepted that a man could not live without artificial aids on the surface of the dusty old planet. But when the first expeditions got there they discovered that the air was considerably richer in oxygen than spectroscopic analysis had ever shown. Still too thin to breathe for very long, of course—a man without a respirator and thermalsuit would be dead in a few hours, and not pleasantly, either. The

27

first colonists had lived in cramped towns huddled under collapsible plastic domes, wearing respirators on those rare occasions when they ventured out of their cocoons. But in time the scientists had found an easier way of doing things, as is usually the case with scientists. But it was not until they perfected the Mishubi-Yakamoto treatments that Earthsiders could move about on Mars without cumbersome tanks or masks. The treatments were lengthy and painful, and, more to the point, they were expensive; but a lone prospector like M'Cord could not exist on Mars without them. It had taken him a couple of years to pay off the medical fees, but it had been worth it.

In deft and subtle ways, the treatments altered human body chemistry so that the body's need for oxygen was considerably lessened and its capacity for using every molecule of the stuff was increased. Subsidiary treatments toughened throat linings and the cellular structure of the lungs so that they took no damage from the dryness and cold. But a man wearied more easily on Mars, despite the reduced weight, and became more susceptible to lung diseases. Even in this, nature found ways to compensate, to balance one loss with another gain: your lungs might go bad on Mars, but your heart was strong as iron.

Right now M'Cord would have happily exchanged his iron heart for a pair of iron legs. He had encountered Thaklar on the Martian equator, at the northernmost tip of the Aram Desert. Following the new direction they had agreed on meant that he had to trek due east about two degrees longitude around the tip of a long, narrow promontory called (for some reason he never knew) the Margaritifer Sinus. Then they turned due south, crossed the central expanse of the Aram, with the interminable rocky wall of the Sinus marching at their right, and still further south and east into the Regio. They got deeper and deeper into the Regio, until, to the north, the ridgeline of the Sabaeus Plateau blocked the entire horizon.

28

M'Cord began to feel like he was going to trudge along forever. For the millionth time he cursed his lack of foresight in not bringing along a pack *slidar* as well as a saddle-beast. Every night, rubbing aching legs, he discovered the existence of muscles he had not known he possessed.

The further they descended into the Regio, the more he puzzled over Thaklar's reasons for wishing to enter this desolate and uninhabited dustland. What conceivable motive would a presumably sane man have for venturing into this powdery hell where even a sandcat couldn't find much food to live on? The native kept his mouth shut about his reasons; he held his secrets to himself, and, despite the grudging comradeship which gradually grew between the two, he shared no confidences with M'Cord.

This new camaraderie came into being in slow and gradual ways. It was not friendship; it was not even the mutual sharing of hardships between two equals. And it was not ever brought out into the open, for the two seldom exchanged words, and when they did it was only to discuss the raw necessities of life.

M'Cord was, by nature, a dour and taciturn man, a man of few words. He kept to himself, had few friends, and never talked about the past. As for the Martian, his hatred of the accursed Earth colonists who had stolen half his world over the last five decades went so deep and strong as to have become almost an instinctive thing by now. Probably he trusted M'Cord by this time as much as he could ever trust a member of his accursed Outworlder race; perhaps he even liked the big man in his grim, somber way. If this thing which grew between them was too tenuous to be called friendship, at least it could be called mutual respect. The sort of thing a strong man feels for another man of equal strength, despite what differences of race or religion or nation stand between

29

them. The sort of thing Kipling was thinking of when he wrote those old lines some two centuries before:

> *Oh, East is East, and West is West, and never the twain shall meet,*
> *Till Earth and Sky stand presently at God's great Judgment Seat.*
> *But there is neither East nor West, Border, nor Breed, nor Birth,*
> *When two strong men stand face to face, though they come from the ends of the earth!*

Part of what grew up between them was that, of course: a man who struggles, endures, and suffers without complaint comes to recognize similar qualities in another man, and is usually smart enough to know the rareness of the quality and the value of it. And there was another thing that bound them together, although neither of them realized it yet; and that was that, under the skin, behind the racial and planetary differences, they were very much the same men.

Both had loved deeply, trusted too much, and both had been betrayed by what they loved. Both had been hurt, terribly hurt, by a woman once. Their hearts wore the same crust of scar tissue from much the same kind of wound. Neither knew it nor even suspected it of the other, but something within them sensed the kinship in the other. And the strange sort of quasi friendship that knit them together existed without words or smiles or confidences, existed in dour silence and brooding, wordless companionship.

In time, the broken bones knit, and knit cleanly. Thaklar could use the leg, but he limped upon it, and it often gave out beneath him. When this happened—as it did rather often, because he forced himself to use the limb—he would lie there cursing in his spitting, sibilant language at the offending leg, while M'Cord sat grinning, waiting for him to get up. Thaklar never knew that M'Cord had been slipping medicine into his rations from the first, chemicals that would fight infection, drive down his fever, and special glandular stimulants designed to greatly accelerate the mending of bones.

This last pharmaceutical had been developed from a Martian cave fungus, and it was crucial to Earthsiders like M'Cord. A broken leg or arm was very nearly the worst thing that could happen to an Earthsider on his own in the wastes, far from the nearest Colonial Administration clinic. It was almost as serious as a broken pressure-still, and M'Cord never ventured very deeply into the dustlands without a plentiful supply of the pharmaceutical. He knew, or guessed, that the stiff-necked warrior would fiercely reject the notion of partaking of any of the ungodly *F'yagha* medicines, had he been apprised of the fact; so M'Cord had simply mixed the stuff into Thaklar's meals from the beginning. The proud native had suspected nothing when M'Cord began making it his habit to prepare their rations; to Thaklar, food making was woman's work, anyway, and he would have resented having to share the task.

And so they went along from day to day. The going was less difficult now, at least for M'Cord. For now that Thaklar's broken leg was mended, they took turns in the saddle while the other walked along before their plodding mount. It was not much easier for Thaklar, plodding through the foot-deep dust, than it had been for the Earthsider. Despite the fact that the Dragon Hawk warrior had been accustomed to these conditions from birth, he found it equally tough going afoot. Except when he is on one of the rock plateaux, a Martian rides on *slidar*back from preference.

But Thaklar knew he must exercise the limb in order to regain the full use of it. It still pained him when he put his full weight upon it, and the muscles of his leg

31

ached abominably from the labor, but he strode along, dragging through the dust of the interminable waste, grim-lipped and uncomplaining.

Except, that is, when the leg gave out suddenly, pitching him into the rolling dust.

On one such occasion he fell with a grunt of pain and lay without moving. M'Cord, riding the *slidar*, thought he had struck his head on a rock and perhaps injured himself. So the Earthman climbed stiffly out of the saddle and went over to see what he could do.

He never got there.

Suddenly, to one side, sand gushed skyward in whirling plumes. An ear-piercing hiss as of escaping steam split the air. It was dusk—the sudden day-to-night transformation that falls so swiftly on Mars, where the atmosphere is too rarified to support such gradations of light as twilight and sunset and the slow deepening of shadows. The far, cold disk of the sun dipped beneath the mountainous horizon, and the sky darkened from dusky purple to jet black in seconds. By the faint light—for neither of the twin moons of Mars shed enough reflected light to be more than dimly half visible in the gloom—M'Cord could not at once make out the cause of this inexplicable dust geyser.

Then a leaping, snarling thing sprang into view—lithe and supple as a panther, with a panther's lashing, whip-like tail, but clad in dully gleaming scales and with the blunt, wedge-shaped skull of a reptile. He knew it in the first blurred glimpse, for it was a sandcat, one of the most dreaded of the predators of the Martian desert country. The creature hollows out its lair beneath the sand, using almost human cunning to tamp the dust into packed-earth walls, then roofs over the narrow entrance with a sandy crust. Therein, like one of Earth's trap-door spiders, the sandcat waits for its prey.

Huger than a kodiak bear, faster than a cheetah, the

32

Martian sandcat is terror incarnate. It strikes like lightning and its ferocity is unparalleled.

And M'Cord had left his gunbelt looped across the saddlehorn.

For the smallest fraction of a second the charging sandcat paused—hesitating between its choice of three dinners. There was the fallen man in the dust, and the man who stood erect with empty hands, and the frightened *slidar,* which screeched and reared around, mad little parrot eyes rolling in mindless fear.

Then it flew at M'Cord like an avalanche, bowling him over, one hideous birdlike claw ripping open his leg from hip to knee. It flung him aside as a child knocks a ragdoll flying, then wheeled in roiling sand—and pounced!

But that brief moment in which it had hesitated between its choice of prey proved to be the beast's undoing. For just as it whirled and sprang upon the stunned and sprawling Earthman, the dark night was split asunder by a blinding noontide glare. A lance of pure blue-white brilliance sprang from the power gun in Thaklar's hand and struck the squalling, scaly fury between the shoulders.

Half stunned from the blow that had felled him, M'Cord lay facedown in the dry, impalpable dust. The flash of the power bolt dazzled his eyes. He blinked through vibrant yellowish-green afterimages at the huge body that lay, twitching spasmodically, kicking up dust with its hind legs. Dazed, he could not quite comprehend what had happened. Thaklar had not been rendered unconscious by his fall, but had lain there in a silent and wordless fury at the failure of his leg, rigid in hate of his own feebleness. An old hand at survival in the dustlands, his fingers were never far from the butt of his gun, even in sleep.

M'Cord blinked, half blind and gasping for breath. The cold air was heavy with the bitter metallic stench of ozone

33

and rank with another odor, too. Only afterward did he identify the rank but not unpleasant aroma as the smell of scorched meat.

Thaklar limped over to where the Earthman lay and examined him wordlessly.

M'Cord was unconscious now. He did not even grunt when the native handled his torn body.

The claws of the sandcat had sliced through the tough, durable nioflex of the thermalsuit as if it had been tissue paper. And they had sliced through the flesh that lay beneath the suiting; the Earthman's leg was slashed from hip to knee. The flesh was laid neatly open as by a surgeon's trained hand, and the massive bone of the upper leg was raw and bare to the eye. Thaklar probed, his fingers gentle as a woman's. The femur did not seem to be broken; not even a fracture could the Martian discern.

But M'Cord was losing blood rapidly, in great gouts, welling out upon the trampled sand as from a water main.

Before so terrible a wound, Thaklar's rude knowledge of the healing arts failed. His hands faltered and fell helplessly to his knees. He squatted by the motionless form of the Earthman, staring down at his unconscious face. His own face was grim and expressionless. His eyes, yellow as the glaring eyes of the sandcat, were unreadable.

But the thoughts which moved behind those eyes were legible:

He saved me from the death of thirst. Now have I not saved him from the jaws of the sandcat? Are not we even, then—one debt erasing the other?

He stared down at M'Cord, eyes fierce and cold as a hawk's.

And is he not one of the accursed F'yagha, for all that he saved me from the thirst? Have not his kind looted and despoiled the world? What more can I do for him, I that know not the healer's skill? Let him die, then; the swift, merciful death. He sleeps; the death of loss of blood

34

will come upon him as he sleeps; he knows not pain in the last sleep. What can I do, even if I would do more?

The Dragon Hawk warrior brooded there in the dark, under the superb stars. Then he rubbed his eyes as if in weariness.

No; he gave me to drink when I lay half dead from thirst. We were strangers, and he gave me to drink. He owed me nothing, then, nor I him. Now there is surely still a debt, for we are no longer strangers.

M'Cord stirred feebly, rubbed dry, dust-caked lips together, and moaned for water. No muscle in Thaklar's hard, lean face moved. He took his own canister from his hip, unsealed it, and set the lip against M'Cord's half-open mouth.

"Share of my water," he said in a low, toneless voice, "brother."

IV. The Road of Millions of Years

After a long time, M'Cord knew that he had awakened and that he was not dead. For surely the dead do not feel pain; and he felt pain.

He blinked open bleared and crusted eyes and looked downward at moving dust. He was bound across the cruppers of the *slidar;* the rank, musky smell of its flesh was heavy in his nostrils. And there was another smell, too—the smell of decay.

From the hips down, his body was afire. His head throbbed; his ribs ached; his lips and the insides of his mouth were dry and coated with dust. He croaked out something in a broken voice and in a moment the beast halted and Thaklar was at his side, loosening the bonds, helping him down to the desert dust. Water was set to his lips and for a while he thought about nothing but the blissful coolness and wetness of it. He took away the can and wiped his mouth and tried to focus on Thaklar's face. The yellow eyes were unreadable, the lean, coppery face inscrutable.

"So I'm still alive," he said inanely.

"You still live," said the other.

"How . . . bad is it, then?"

"It is bad, my brother. See for yourself."

M'Cord made no comment on Thaklar's use of the word "brother"; he knew what it meant, or what it probably implied. But there were more serious things to think about. He looked down at himself and, after a while, he looked away sickly.

"How long has it been?" he muttered after a while. The desert man told him the number of days. M'Cord licked his lips and tried to think. A man does not live long in the desert unless he knows a thing or two about the body. Thaklar had done the best he knew: he had staunched the wound as much as it could be staunched, and he had wound a tourniquet tightly about M'Cord's upper thigh between the crotch and the hip, cutting off the circulation.

He had even known enough to loosen the tourniquet from time to time. But he knew nothing about the medicines in the kit, and probably would have scorned to use them even had he known. M'Cord lay there and thought about blood poisoning for a while, sweating and sick to the stomach. Then he asked for the kit, for more water, and for a blanket to keep out the dust.

There were powerful, broad-spectrum bactericides in the kit, and an anticlotting agent, and tubes of neomycin IV. M'Cord took three pain-killers and a tablet of caffein concentrate to clear his head. Then he gave himself several injections, starting with twelve cubic centimeters of energol. That was just on this side of the tolerance limit, but it would keep him going for three hours without pain or fatigue. He would pay the price afterward, he knew; but right now he had work to do. The energol spread through him like a cloud of tingling fire: pain dimmed and vanished, he felt sharp and clear and steady. He began to work on the leg.

38

Thaklar had not cleansed the wound. In the dustlands, one does not wash anything, even a wound, with water. Water is rarer and more precious than blood; more precious even than life. And the whole of the long, hideous gash was crusted with clotted blood and dust. M'Cord cleaned it out with a damp swab made of a rag, then smeared in the neomycin, covered it with gel, and began to sew up the wound as best he could. The shots kept him from feeling anything at all but he knew what he was doing and he had to crush his lips tight and clamp his jaws together to keep from vomiting. The fleshy edges of the gash were purple-black and puffy. He slashed them open with a scalpel and let the pus drain, then swabbed them with the neomycin and sewed them up. From time to time he stopped to rest, and drank a few mouthfuls of precious brandy. He knew he didn't have much of a chance, but there was nothing else to do but try.

Thaklar had bound the wound shut with strips torn from a blanket, knit tight, holding the ragged edges of the thermalsuit closed as best as could be done. If it hadn't been for that, there would have been frostbite to contend with.

When he was done, it was nearly nightfall, so they made camp and ate a meal. M'Cord had no appetite but he forced himself to down the meat stew and took more pills. He had several hours of pain-free lucidity left, he knew, before the fever and the raving began, if they were going to begin, and he very much feared they were. He showed Thaklar the different pills and rehearsed him in the few simple acts the other would have to do, once M'Cord was unable to do them himself.

They spoke few words while eating. Finally:

"It is bad, 'Gort." It was not a question. M'Cord nodded.

"It is bad," he grunted. "You will have to tie me when

he raving starts, or I will wander off in the night. And I will beg you for water; but you must give me only this much a day, up to here," he said, measuring with his fingers. The other nodded somberly.

"I did the best I could, 'Gort."

M'Cord nodded. "I know. Thanks." There was really nothing else to say. For four days and nights the warrior had fed him and cared for him and cleaned him when he soiled himself. There were no words with which to thank a man for such kindness.

They were midway into the Regio by now. Soon, perhaps tomorrow, Thaklar meant to head north into the Sabaeus. By then M'Cord would be half mad with the fever and would know nothing. A day or two more and he might well be dead. They were both aware of it; they did not discuss it.

There was a strange expression on Thaklar's face; its bleakness softened. He was trying to say something and it came hard. M'Cord lay there, empty and weary, feeling the numbness and euphoric comfort ebb as the pain began, and waited for him to speak, if he meant to speak. M'Cord didn't give a damn whether he opened up or not.

Then, finally:

"I have shared water with you; I did it while you slept."

"I know it, brother," said M'Cord. Something very much like a smile flickered across the stern features of the other man.

"It is written that a man must not keep secrets from his brother. 'Gort, I would tell you who I am and how I am come to this place, and what I would do."

M'Cord nodded and waited silently.

When the story came out, it was even stranger than he had thought it would be.

40

The Dragon Hawk nation are a proud and ancient people. The blood of kings flows in their veins, attenuated by many ages, it is true, but nonetheless royal.

Thaklar was a High Prince of his people, or had been once. His was an ancient House—ancient even for a race whose princes can often trace their lineage back a million years to the early Pleistocene.

Once—long ago, before the oceans receded and the air thinned and the blue forests and plains died to powdery sand—they were a mighty civilization. From pole to pole the word of the Jamad Tengru, the pope-emperor, was holy law. There were ten nations then, ten mighty clans numbering in the many millions. But then the world began to die; and they to die with it.

As the briny seas shrank, exposing miles of muddy shoreline, the marble seaport cities were left behind to crumble in decay. Vast populations became homeless wanderers as their fields and forests withered into dust. Much was lost in the chaotic ages that followed: the science they had once had from their gods, the wisdom they had preserved over interminable aeons. They became nomads; then barbarians; then little more than savages.

But they were a proud and ancient people, and they were stubborn. They adapted to a dying world; hardship and deprivation toughened them. They survived. And they clung to what little could be preserved of their ancient lore and wisdom.

Scattering far apart, separated by thousands of square miles of deserts that had once been the floors of vanished seas, losing touch with one another, each of the nine nations whose remnants had survived into the twilight of the planet guarded its own hoarded scraps of knowledge. The possession of these fragments of ancient wisdom became hereditary. The guardianship of this knowledge was handed down from father to son through many millennia.

Thus it was with the House of Thaklar.

And there on the desert plain, huddled together for warmth under the frozen stars, the Martian princeling told his secret to the Earthman who had become, so strangely, so unexpectedly, his brother.

"From of old, brother, my House has guarded the secret of the Road of Millions of Years. To us it has been given by the Timeless Ones to guard forever the way to the *huatan*. You who have read The Book and who know somewhat of our lore, will know, perhaps, what is meant by that word."

M'Cord regarded him puzzledly. Of course, he knew enough of the Tongue to know that *huatan* meant "sacred valley." But he was no scholar; something he knew of the Epics and the Chronicles, but his knowledge was limited to little more than may be gleaned from listening to a bard chant the old songs to a circle of listening nomads around a heat unit under the glittering stars.

The sacred valley . . .

Something stirred at the back of his mind, some old, half-forgotten scrap of lore. He tried to recall it to memory; but now Thaklar was speaking again. His lean face was grim, his hawk-fierce eyes were bleak with an old hurt.

"To me in my turn was the secret given. The secret my forefathers had guarded from the beginnings of time itself. And from me was it stolen. And by a *woman*."

The last word was spat out as if it left a vile taste on his tongue. The Martian brooded, his face cold and hard, hugging his knees somberly.

"Her name was Zerild. She was a Low Clan woman who danced before men for gold. She came to the encampment of my nation in a caravan of fat merchants, and she danced before us in the starlight, and she was . . .

42

very beautiful. I desired her as a thirsty man desires water; but she laughed at me and denied me her body. That I might slake my thirst I offered her riches and a place in my House. A place of honor. And still she denied me, and yet again she laughed."

His head sank upon his broad chest and his face was turned away so that M'Cord could not read his expression. Not that he needed to.

"There was a madness came upon me then. Never have I been a weakling for women; never has Thaklar of the Dragon Hawk nation groveled before the feet of a woman; never have I been a slave to the hunger of my loins. But before the slender body of the woman Zerild I was as one gripped by the spell of an enchanter. I became bereft of reason, of honor. She taunted me, laughing, swaying before me, her eyes like great gems flashing through the silken curtain of her night-black hair. I hungered for her breasts, that were like golden fruit. I was famished for the touch of her . . . and, in my madness and my folly, I bade her ask of me what she would. She asked of me nothing, she said, but a token that my love for her was stronger than all other loves my heart held. She asked of me the secret the princes of my blood had held sacred from the birth of time. She asked that I reveal to her the way to Ophar the Holy . . . *aiyee,* my brother! Would that I had died a coward's death in that moment, before my lips could open, as they did open, and I could yield to her that which she desired! But I did not die."

A cold chill went through M'Cord's blood as he listened to the slow, tortured words the other whispered there under the cold glitter of the stars.

For now that elusive scrap of memory that had stirred in the depths of his mind had risen up within him. And now he knew what it was that the other had meant by *huatan*—the sacred valley. He understood what Thaklar had been talking about, and he knew, or thought he knew,

43

what the secret had been that the Hawk princes of Thaklar's line had guarded so carefully and for so long.

With a faint horror he realized what it was that the warrior at his side had done that had earned him the contempt of his clan brethren and lifelong exile from their camps.

He had betrayed the way to the Garden of Eden out of desire for a woman's body.

V. To the Gates of Ygnarh

They went on with dawn, marching north toward the plateau. They spoke few words between them, for the fever was growing in M'Cord and the pain was there within him like a small burning fire. As for Thaklar, a black mood of murderous depression was upon him and he strode along wearily, head bent, thinking his own thoughts.

M'Cord pitied him, even in his own torment. For he understood the enormity of Thaklar's sin.

Ophar, or "The Holy," as it is called, is the Eden of the religion of the natives of Mars. The Valley Where Life Was Born, they call it. It was there, in this mysterious and sacrosanct Valley, according to myths that are older than the mountains, that the Timeless Ones first created life. It was in that secret place that the Martian Adam was molded from the flesh of beasts, was shaped to manhood, and was given that spark of immortality that distinguishes the man from the beast.

But it is more than just the cradle of the race; for The Holy hides within its breast the most precious of all the many gifts the Timeless Ones bestowed upon their foster-children. And that is the *Jhay yam-i-Jaah* itself, the Pool of Eternity which contains the Water of Life. Think of it as the Martian equivalent of the Fountain of Youth, which that grizzled and gullible old soldier-of-fortune, Ponce de Leon, once searched for in the fever-swamps of Florida, and you will not be far off the mark.

This was all legend and myth, of course, and M'Cord knew it. It was the stuff of fairy tales. M'Cord had seen too much of life to believe in any man's gods—not even those of his own people, and certainly not the strange gods of an alien planet. But holiness is a measure of reverence and awe which men hold for certain symbols and stories, and it has nothing to do with fact or truth or the real world. Men need their myths as they need their heroes: it is necessary to believe in something greater than oneself to avoid yielding to disgust and contempt for everything, including oneself.

For some the holy thing, the sacred thing, is Home or Flag or Country. For other men it is a way of life, a creed or a political system or an ethical standard. But for many men it is a collection of old, age-neglected tales in a Book. M'Cord had no faith in the Book, whether it be the Book of his own Christian ancestors or the Book of the Martian religion. But he knew how much it meant to them, the dwindling remnants of a dying people. And he understood at last the full horror of what Thaklar had done.

The rest of the story leaked from Thaklar's tight lips in bits and pieces over the next two days. He had told the secret to the dancing girl to prove that his love for her was stronger even than his hereditary vows, stronger than his honor. And before he had clasped her in his arms even once, she had fled in the night on a stolen *slidar,* and was gone into the trackless wastes. She had only toyed with him, as a cat toys with a helpless small thing, cruelly, playfully, with sharp claws sheathed in soft velvet until the final moment of truth.

M'Cord did not believe that even Thaklar held the ancient myths to be true. But that did not matter in the least. It was enough to know that he had betrayed the honor of his House for a taunting, laughing wanton. He had spat upon the graves of his ancestors. He had sold the precious treasure of his fathers for the flesh of a woman, which is a sin infinitely more despicable than to have sold it for power or gold. He had gone that very hour before the old Prince of his nation to confess his sin, which was beyond redemption as it was beyond punishment. His name had been taken from him there, and the princedom of his House had been cast down in the dust. A nameless, tribeless wanderer, he had been driven forth from the camps of his people to walk the world in bitter loneliness until death came for him.

There was no longer anything for him to live for. But there was one thing, one desire he nourished in his heart that was fiercer and deeper even than had been his desire for the woman.

And the name of it was Revenge.

M'Cord was stronger and tougher than even he, himself, had dreamed. He had thought the fever would come upon him in hours, but his blood fought and held the sickness at bay for two days. At last, however, his strength failed him and he sank into the raving madness. Thaklar tended him, fed him, gave him water, and bound him to the saddle so that he could not fall. And into the food and drink he mixed the medicines as M'Cord had bidden him during the time when he had been lucid. He followed these instructions although he placed no credence in the medicines of the Outworlders.

At night, bone-weary, he huddled by M'Cord and talked to him in low, quiet tones. The Earthman was

47

gaunt and wasted by now, and his eyes were bright with madness; he writhed and raved in his bonds.

Thaklar talked to him because there was nothing else to talk to but the desert and the silence, the night and the stars. Perhaps he thought the sound of a human voice might soothe and calm M'Cord in his madness. And perhaps it did, a little. But it is more than likely that he talked merely to unburden his soul and keep himself sane.

He had wandered the world over (he told M'Cord), searching for the dancer Zerild. He sought her in the encampments of the People, and among the caravans of the fat merchants, and even among the despised *F'yagha*, in the native quarter of the Earth colonies.

He sought word of her everywhere; but he learned nothing and he found her not.

Then it had occurred to him, with a cold thrill of unholy fear, that mayhap she had not wheedled the secret from him merely to satisfy her sense of power over him, but for gain and for a purpose.

The only purpose his mind could envision was the old, familiar reason—the motive which drove men on every world to search for the Unobtainable. The motive which drove the old Spanish *conquistadores* to explore the wilderness of unknown America for their own Fountain of Youth. And the name of that motive was the fear of death, of growing old. For it was written in The Book that whoso drank of the Pool would become young and strong again, never to age and never to die.

And a woman like Zerild, who earns her gold by tempting men with her beauty and by flaunting her youthfulness before their lust, fears nothing so much as age, with its silver hairs and its wrinkled flesh.

Now the first step on the Road of Millions of Years was in the city called Ygnarh.

It was old, that city: older than the Carboniferous. So old that even the legends did not recall when first its pillars

48

had been raised against the sky. It had died so long ago that even the Epics did not remember a time when it had been the habitation of men. "The first of cities," it was named in The Book; it was like the Land of Nod, wherein had Adam settled first when he had been driven to the east of Eden and that gates of paradise were closed behind him by an angel with a sword of fire.

If ever there had truly been a city called Ygnarh, Thaklar believed that he would find it in the Sabaeus Sinus Plateau. This had been part of the secret his family had guarded from time immemorial; and the reason why the Road of Millions of Years had been kept secret was to prevent men from seeking Ophar the Holy wherein lay the Water of Life, for to bathe therein would be blasphemy. Very long ago the gods decreed that it was not good for a man to live forever, or to dwell in the Valley Beyond Time, where once the gods themselves had walked. So the way thereunto was forbidden and the road was made secret, and the guardianship of that secret was given into the hands of the founder of the House of Thaklar.

From that day to this, no man of that House had revealed the secret to an outsider; when the father lay dying, then and then only was the secret whispered to his eldest son. Thus it had been for ages. And only Thaklar had betrayed that ancient trust.

He could never win forgiveness for his sin, he knew. But he could slay the woman who had coaxed it from him, and forever close her lips in silence. That would at very least satisfy him; it would do much to remove the burden of guilt which weighed like lead upon his spirit. And to that purpose he had devoted himself. He had been bound for Ygnarh when his beast had collapsed beneath him, pinning him down there in the Aram, where the Outworlder who was now his brother had found him.

Why the beast had died he never knew. It was the way of *slidars,* who can lope strong and tireless and uncomplaining for hundreds of leagues. When they have reached the end of their strength, they die all at once, as if struck down. It is the way of *slidars*.

M'Cord's beast succumbed on the third day. Suddenly it uttered a blood-chilling hiss and came to its knees, head lolling drunkenly. Alarm flashed through Thaklar, rousing him from his weary stupor. He sprang forward, a hooked knife glinting naked in his fist. Barely had he cut the unconscious figure of M'Cord loose from his bonds and dragged him from the saddle when the *slidar* fell over on its side in the dust and lay there panting for a few moments before it died.

Thaklar stared at the dead beast, then raised his eyes to the mountainous wall of the plateau that marched across the horizon to the north. It looked near; it looked very near. But he knew it was not, and his heart quailed within him.

He could carry the saddlebags, because he must. Therein were stored the food and the water, the blankets and the medicines.

But he could not carry M'Cord.

Even gaunt and wasted and shrunken with fever, the Earthman was a cumbersome burden. And Thaklar knew that his broken leg, although it was healed by now, was not strong enough to bear that burden.

But there was nothing else to do but—try.

Little enough of his tarnished honor remained to him. That little he clung to with all the strength and determination he possessed. And never should it be said of Thaklar of the Dragon Hawk nation that he had left a brother behind to die in the dustlands, while he went forth, alone, to live.

He bent over the dead beast and removed the saddlebags with some difficulty, since they were partly pinned under the carcass.

Then he judiciously searched through their meager

50

stores, discarding everything that could safely be dispensed with, everything that was not absolutely vital to their survival.

That which remained he bundled up in the leather bag and slung it about him, clipping it to the rings of his harness so that it hung down upon his breast.

Then he bent down, gently picked up M'Cord, and slung the unconscious man over his shoulders, adjusting the weight until he could bear it comfortably.

"Very well then, my brother," he said harshly. "From henceforward I shall be thy riding-beast. And live or die, we shall meet our fate together. . . ."

He walked off into the north with the Earthman on his back.

The plateau was nearer now, but not near enough. He could reach it within three days, he thought; in three days, if the old tales told true, he would enter the gates of Ygnarh.

But whether M'Cord would live that long, only the Timeless Ones knew.

VI. Zerild

It was a dream, M'Cord thought; always the same dream. But this one was strangely different. . . .

The dust, the endless drifts of powdery ochre dust, were gone as if swept away by a magician's word. In place of the dust was naked rock, pitted and scored and crumbling and very old. The rock closed about him in steep, towering walls that narrowed like the jaws of a vise.

And then, just as he dreamed the jaws of the vise would close upon him, they opened, quite suddenly, into a wide and open place that lay naked beneath the sun.

And in that place there stood a city.

It was very old, that city. Older than man's memory; older even than man's dreams.

It was the skeleton of a city, really. Crumbling walls that still stood, although their domed roofs had fallen in; pillars that leaned crazily awry, or lay fallen and shattered and moldering into dust.

The gates still stood, by some jest of time or fate. The gates and the pillars of the gates still rose up, stern and forbidding, although the walls of the city themselves had long ago fallen to break and sunder and lapse into the detritus of the ages.

That which bore him on its back—the haggard, stumbling scarecrow of a man—lurched through the gates, which hung open.

Down a long avenue of paving stones he staggered. It was lined on either side with houses, or the remains of them. Like sun-bleached skulls, they were, the houses; mere empty shells with hollow windows that gaped black and empty as the eye sockets and unbarred portals that yawned like the opened jaws.

Everywhere was dust and desolation and scattered stones and the bare bones of fallen towers. Oh, it was a strange dream, this one! M'Cord tried to laugh at its craziness, but he could not, for his tongue was black and swollen.

In the central plaza the buildings still stood to the height of two or three stories. They had been built to last, these palaces or temples or whatever they once had been; and their stout walls of pale amber marble had stood strong against the remorseless erosion of a million years and more.

That which bore him set him down there in the shadow of a wall, and knelt beside him and set water to his lips. It was precious, that water, more precious than gold or even blood, and few were the drops that were left. They shared it between them, the scarecrow and the corpse that dreamed it was still alive.

Then they rested until the others came.

When they heard the scrape of boot-leather against dusty stone, the scarecrow staggered to its feet again, one claw-like hand on the butt of its gun, but it was too late, for the muzzles of three energy guns stared at them fixedly, like cold, black, unwavering eyes.

Slowly Thaklar let his hand fall and dropped the pistol to the pave.

The others stared at him and at the sprawled corpse-like figure of M'Cord with hard, cold, thoughtful, measuring eyes for a long, long moment of tension and aching silence.

The first of them, who must have been their leader, judging from his stance, was a lean, rangy wolf of a man. A Low Clan warrior, with seamed leathery face and hard, small, suspicious eyes. He wore two bandoliers which criss-crossed his broad, hard-muscled chest, and a gun sat in its holster on each hip, and a thick black whip with a worn silver handle hung coiled there, as well. In his dark capable hands he held an electric rifle of *F'yagha* manu-facture. He held it with that casual ease borne of long familiarity and use. He knew how to use it, Thaklar knew, and he might very well use it at any moment.

The other man was small and stunted like a dwarf, and gaunt in the ribs, and very old. His furcap was shaven and he wore sigils of silver clipped to his ear-lobes, like a priest. But he, too, wore the leathern tunic and harness of a warrior, not the billowing robes of an ecclesiastic. If the face of the leader was lean and hard and dangerous as a wolf's, the small man's face was like that of a snake. In-deed, the resemblance was uncanny: the same blunt, wedge-shaped brow; the same narrow, tapering, chinless face; and the same cold, unblinking, lidless eyes, empty of all save ferocity.

He hissed a word to his companion between thin lips. And as he did so, Thaklar half fancied he saw the pointed tip of a forked tongue flicker out to moisten dry lips.

The third of the party stood to one side in the shadow of a pillar which had everything but the long barrel of the rifle which was pointed directly at his heart.

He ignored the others, and met the cunning, suspicious eyes of the wolf-like one, holding them with his own.

It was a moment of indecision: a moment of wavering

and of trial. It was also a good moment for a bluff, and Thaklar knew it.

These men were outlaws, he knew. They wore no clan markings and their garments were unfringed with the tartan-like patterns that are as heraldic blazons to the Martians. Outlaws or outcasts, with the hand of every man raised against them. They feared him because he was an unknown factor; and they feared him because they could not be certain he was alone.

It was a moment that could easily and swiftly end in death, he knew. It was a moment to put fear behind him and to don a casual and fearless stance. But he was afraid, was Thaklar. Any man would have felt fear there in the empty, lifeless square under the dull blaze of the sun, pinned like a moth between the pointing muzzles of the three guns.

But the blood of ancient kings flowed in the veins of Thaklar, and the pride of an ancient heritage stiffened his spine. He would die if he must, but he would not show fear in the face of death. He drew himself up proudly and folded his arms upon his breast and matched the wolf-like man stare for stare. And when he spoke, his words were calm and measured, and his voice did not tremble in the slightest.

"You need not fear me. My guns are at my feet and I am alone, save for the man there, who is half dead of fever. And I am an outlaw, like yourself."

The wolf-faced man sucked in his breath between bared teeth, whistling sharply. His eyes glittered warily beneath the shadow of his *kaffira* headdress.

"Who is this that knows Chastar, but upon whom the eyes of Chastar have never rested before?" he demanded. His voice was fierce and high and tight with suspicion.

Thaklar shrugged indifferently.

"I know you not, nor have we ever met, to my certain

56

knowledge. But who would dwell here in a dead city in the middle of nowhere but one with a price on his head?"

The glint of suspicion seemed to dim a trifle as Thaklar's words went home. It was as much the casual, uncaring tone in which they were spoken as it was the import of the words that dulled those suspicious fires.

The man who called himself Chastar said in a harsh voice: "Kick your gun over here with your foot, and make no sudden moves." Thaklar calmly did as he was bidden. Still without taking his eyes off Thaklar, the outlaw said to the dwarfish little man whose head was shaven like a priest's, "You. Pick it up."

The priest hissed wordlessly, bobbed his head, and scuttled over to snatch up Thaklar's pistol. Chastar took it from him and examined the weapon. It bore no clan crest, for it had been purchased from a smuggler in the back alleys of Yeolarn. He grunted something and thrust it within his belt.

"Who are you and how did you get here?" he demanded harshly.

"My name is Thaklar, and I walked most of the way."

Chastar opened his mouth as if to challenge that, but then his eyes narrowed as he took in, perhaps for the first time, the worn and weary and dust-laden condition of Thaklar's clothing.

His eyes fell next to the half-conscious Earthman at Thaklar's feet. He indicated him with a nod.

"What is that you have with you? Are you a friend to the accursed Outworlders, or perhaps in their pay?"

Thaklar shook his head stiffly.

"I bear no love for the *F'yagha*—as a race. But the man who lies here in the shadow of death, although it is true he is a *F'yagh*, is my friend. My brother."

Without speaking, the other man studied him with cold, curious eyes. He suspected that there were words left unspoken; he hesitated.

"Thaklar—that is your name? But you do not name your nation," he observed.

Thaklar said: "No more than you name yours, and for the same reason. Because I have no nation; I am *aoudh*. An outlaw, as I have already told you."

"He lies," a clear, sweet voice sang from the shadows.

At the sound of that voice Thaklar froze and his grim face went pale.

Now the third of the band stepped forth from the shadow of the pillar into the open sunlight.

It was a woman. A girl, really, from her shallow pointed breasts and long, slim, coltish legs. Her hair was a banner of black silk flung carelessly back over strong, slender shoulders to pour down her spine like a cataract of glittering ink. Her face was heart-shaped, elfin, with broad cheekbones, slanted eyes, and a small, pointed chin. It was a mask of tawny, smooth loveliness, that face, with a wide, full-lipped mouth on which malicious laughter sat enthroned. There was mischief in the immense sparkling eyes that flashed like wet jewels under thick lashes. She was beautiful, the girl; she was very beautiful. Even in the dreamlike stupor of his fever, the manhood in M'Cord responded to the promise and the tempting allure in that beauty.

She strolled out into the sun-lit plaza, lazy and languid, like a slim, tawny cat. The eyes of the men were upon her, and she knew it. She basked in their gaze.

Holding their eyes, she stretched and arched her slim, supple back, and yawned a small, pink-mouthed little kitten yawn. Her eyes twinkled as she took in her audience with a quick flicker of a glance; then thick lashes fell demurely, masking her gaze.

Chastar stood regarding her with baffled, wary puzzlement. The little priestling watched her appraisingly, his eyes drawn into slits. But Thaklar stood as one thunder-

58

struck, his face frozen into an expressionless mask of cold bronze.

Only his lips moved, whispering a name. The word fell into the silence, which absorbed it as sun-baked dust drinks up a droplet of moisture. The others did not hear that name, but M'Cord heard it.

The name was ... *Zerild.*

VII. The Empty Place on the Map

It was a curious tableau, the sun bright but shedding no heat, the worn, crumbling, ancient stones, and the motionless group.

Sprawled in the shadow of the wall, M'Cord felt somehow detached from it all. He was a mere spectator, while the others were the actors in this little drama.

For a moment the girl held them with her witchery. But then the moment passed.

"I say again: he lies," the girl said, smiling. There was mischief and mockery in her eyes. She grinned at them all; then she turned away.

Chastar was tense and nervous. He turned upon her swiftly, his eyes hard and wary again.

"What is it that you would say? Speak, woman, and have done with these hints and mockeries!"

"Yes. How does he lie, lady?" murmured the hunched little old man with the shaven pate. He still held the gun clenched in knotted, ugly hands. The muzzle of that gun pointed directly at Thaklar's heart. And it did not waver.

Thaklar stood impassively, arms folded upon his breast. His face was devoid of any expression at all.

61

The girl shrugged.

"A lie is a lie," she said.

Chastar spat and swore viciously.

"Do you know this man, slut? Speak! Answer me, Zerild, or I will lay your back open with the whip. Do you know this man?"

She looked at him and laughed.

"You will not touch me with that great whip of yours, for if you do, then you will never learn from me the way to The Holy. So watch your tongue and mind your manners, red wolf, or you will lock my lips on silence, if you are not careful, and I will seek another to go with me to the Valley."

"Curse you, wench!" the outlaw snarled. "You will strangle yourself with that tireless tongue of yours, someday. Now answer with no more foolishness: do you know this man or don't you?"

Her lazy, mocking eyes turned to meet the stony gaze of Thaklar.

Then they looked away.

"We have met," she said, shrugging carelessly.

"Well, then? You say he lies—what is the lie, curse you!" Chastar spat. Dreaming, M'Cord knew somehow that they were constantly at each other's throats, the wolf-man and the cat-woman; the love between them—if they were indeed lovers—must be a wild, furious thing of claw scratches and brutal buffets.

She lifted one slim hand to toy with the little copper bells woven in her hair. They chimed faintly, making soft, whispering music whenever she moved.

"He is a prince of the Dragon Hawk nation," she said indifferently. "Or, at least, he was when I knew him." Something unspoken hung behind her words. Chastar began breathing heavily; the smell of male jealousy was heavy in the air, like sour musk.

"He had you? You were lovers, then? *Speak*, you silken tormentor!" he cried out, his voice harsh and raw and thick with murderous fury. She eyed him lazily, coolly, eyes faintly disdainful.

"If you prefer to think so," she said.

"I know it; I can taste in on the air," growled Chastar, breathing heavily. There was murder in his eyes now, and the hands that held the gun shook with the intensity of his emotion.

The man was strung too taut, M'Cord thought dreamily. His nerves were raw, exposed. The slightest touch stung him to fury. And the dancing girl played with him like this—taunting him, teasing him? It was like playing with a naked razor.

"If you like," Zerild shrugged. "But the truth of the matter is that he has never once touched me—no, not so much as to lay his hand upon me. Not that he did not wish to, and very strongly. Almost as strongly as you, Chastar." Mockery sparkled in her eyes until the lashes veiled them again.

The odd thing was that her words seemed to calm the wolfish outlaw. Perhaps it was that he knew she always spoke the truth, or perhaps it was merely that he wished from the very roots of his soul to believe her. At any rate, the murderous fury faded from his burning eyes and he grew calmer. Indeed, a sardonic humor welled up from within him; he looked Thaklar over from head to foot, and laughed a little. It was an ugly laugh—cruel and gloating.

"Ah! Now I understand It! He is the princeling from whom you tricked the secret of the Road, eh, wench? Well, why didn't you say so in the first place? *Faugh!* You are a sly and devious slut, upon my honor! Well, princeling; and how does it feel to have been the dupe of a woman like her, eh?"

Thaklar was sweating under his tunic, but he remained poised and outwardly cool. The emotional tensions be-

63

tween these persons were subtle and complex—too complex to be grasped easily. He shrugged, ignoring the malice behind the bantering tone.

"You know how it feels, Chastar," he grinned. "I think she dupes you, too. Or have you had better luck than I, and actually got your money's worth—in bed?"

That stung the outlaw. He swore and took an impulsive step forward, one hand falling to the butt of the whip which hung coiled at his waist.

Then Zerild laughed—a silvery music, cold and lovely.

"He has had no more of me than have you, O Hawk!" she said. "And it has chafed him raw. Oh, you men; you men! You must forever be trying to possess something, to own it, to grapple it to you with chains or oaths or promises! But I am Zerild—a free woman! I do not give myself lightly, but when I give, I give utterly."

"And do you ever give, then?" asked Thaklar.

The girl laughed, flaunting her vivid beauty before him. For a moment her eyes met his, freely, joyously, as if sensing a kindred spirit. Then the little witch-lights of mockery danced in them again and they turned cruel.

"I have never given myself to a man yet; for I have yet to meet the man worthy of the gift! Know, O Hawk, that when I do meet such a man, he will have all of me. You others, wolf-Chastar and your ilk, all you will ever have of me is a glimpse—a whisper of my laugh—a wisp of perfume on the air!"

Chastar stared at her hotly.

"I will have you when I want you. I have told you that. I—*take* what I want. You shall be mine, Zerild!"

"Perhaps," she yawned. "And perhaps not. But anyway, that was not part of the bargain. You are to make easeful my road to The Holy; and I am to be the signpost that tells you the way. And we are to share the treasure that we shall find there together, you and I. As for any-

64

thing else, it was not in the pact. If it shall happen between us, then it shall happen. If not, then it shall not."

Chastar turned to regard Thaklar.

"So you followed the wench here, eh, princeling? The taste of cuckoldry is bitter on the tongue, eh?"

"Not cuckoldry," said Thaklar, smiling. "For you took from me nothing which ever once I possessed. She has told the truth in that, at least, wolf. Nor does it seem you have her yet. But I did not follow her; I came here thinking that I might find her here. And I came alone."

"For revenge—is that the name of it?"

"Some might call it that. But I have another name for it."

Chastar made an impatient gesture as if to shove all of this away from him.

"I grow weary of all this wagging-of-tongues. What shall we do with them, eh, Phuun?"

The little priest regarded the two with flat eyes, hard and dull.

"Kill them, lord. What else?"

Chastar grinned viciously—a wolfish leer that bared his long teeth as a snarl would bare them. But before he could speak, Thaklar laughed. The unexpectedness of the reaction made the outlaw pause; he blinked puzzledly.

"Now, here is another marvel! First we have a man who follows a woman he hates halfway across the world—and not for revenge. And now he laughs in the very mouth of death! Riddle me this wonder, priest!"

"I will riddle it for you," Thaklar said. "The Road is unfinished."

The words hung there in the sun-baked silence. Chastar blinked.

Zerild turned back to face them, hands on slim, rounded hips.

"He lies again, Chastar. Kill him now, wolf, for we cannot take the Road with an enemy among us. He will slay us all while we sleep, for only thus may he redeem his error in yielding the secret unto me. Kill him, wolf, and perhaps I will love you for it—a little, anyway!"

"You will not take the Road at all, woman, because you do not know the way," Thaklar said calmly.

Chastar turned his gaze upon Zerild.

"Now, by the gods, woman, have you lied to me after all? Know you the way to Ophar, or don't you?"

Thaklar laughed boldly, and sat down in the shadows. "Ah, wolf, you have trusted a woman who betrays men because she loves to do so; and now you, too, have been betrayed! Is it possible, then, that she has never shown you the map? I see by the look in your face that thus it is. Well, there is one part missing from that map—one portion left blank. And only I know what should be written there; therefore, if you slay me, you shall never reach the Valley and live to tell the tale. Ask her to show it to you, if you think I lie."

Chastar glowered upon Zerild, and she shrank from meeting his gaze and bit her lip in vexation. The priest kept his gun trained on Thaklar and M'Cord; but he watched the outlaw and his woman with cold and hungry eyes.

"Is this true?" Chastar breathed between his teeth.

"It is true . . . there is a blank spot on the map . . . but—"

"But—*what?*"

"But the—the silver is worn and frail and very old, and I . . . I thought that the markings were merely rubbed away. . . ."

"And that is where you made your mistake, woman," Thaklar said softly from the shadows. "For my ancestors knew well that, guard a treasure however you will, there will always be men clever enough to steal it in the end. So they left part of the secret chart unmarked, and that which should have been marked there was handed down from

66

father to son in spoken words, whispered from the death-bed. You can never reach Ophar alive, unless I go with you to tell you the way."

"How can we trust you, knowing that you are the guardian of that which we have contrived to steal? You will trick us all into the jaws of death, to keep the secret safe," snarled Chastar.

Thaklar calmly watched his working face and furious eyes.

"That, Chastar, is your problem. You must find a way to convince me that you will not have me slain the moment we are past the place where only I can guide you."

Chastar stared at him blankly.

"Do you mean to say—you will go with us, to the Valley?"

Even Zerild stared with amazement at the princeling. He laughed and stretched wearily.

"What else is there to do?"

"But *why?*" demanded the outlaw.

Thaklar shrugged. "Perhaps because I am as curious as any other man, and would know the truth behind the old story. Or because, like any other man, I hunger to live forever—eternally young, eternally strong."

He sat up, rubbing his face.

"But now—let us have done with talking for a while. Let it be a truce between us, for a little. You have my word as a prince of the High Blood that I shall not attempt to slay you when your backs are turned. I am weary and would rest; hunger and thirst quarrel together in my belly, so that even I cannot say which yowls the loudest. And my brother here is very weak and ill with the sickness; are there medicines here, or be one of you a healer—the priest, perhaps?"

"There is a *F'yagha* healer in our camp," muttered Chastar, nodding to the ruined palace across the plaza. "My prisoner; he will have medicines. Phuun—take them hence and see them locked within with the Hated Ones. My brain whirls with all these words. We will speak together when we dine, princeling. Come, woman! I would see this precious map of yours at last, to make certain how much of your words have been lies!"

They left the square, Chastar and the dancing girl, and Phuun, nudging with the barrel of his gun, indicated the far building. With a groan of weary muscles, Thaklar bent and took up the burden of his brother once again and carried him into the building.

As for M'Cord, this latest and strangest dream of all faded as the brief spell of lucidity blurred into the red murk of nightmare again, and he sank back into the hot embrace of the fever.

And when he next emerged to wakefulness, it was to look up into the face of an angel.

II

THE ROAD
TO
OPHAR

VIII. A Time of Healing

At least, she looked like an angel to a man who had seen
no women but wine-shop sluts and back-alley wenches for
more years than he cared to count. Her hair was cornsilk
yellow, tied back with a scrap of cloth, tumbling about
the nape of her neck in careless, shining curls. The thermalsuit she wore was old and stained and loose-fitting;
but even it could not really conceal the slim, strong lines of
her body nor the rounded fullness of her breasts.

Her eyes were blue. There were lines of strain about
them, and shadow stains of weariness. And there was pain
in them, an old pain, and a haunting guilt. They puzzled
him, those eyes. The eyes of angels should be pure and
candid and guilt-free.

She was bathing his brows with a piece of scrap cloth
soaked in astringent cleanser when he opened his eyes
and looked up into her face. For a moment she did not
notice that he was awake, nor did he realize that she was
real. He lay there, blissfully relaxed, weak to the point
of being feeble, but free of pain. Even the fever had
drained from him: his mind was clear enough, but empty.
And the pain in his leg, which he had lived with so long

that by now it seemed like part of him—the pain was gone.

He wished he could see her mouth. It would be soft and full-lipped, tender and vulnerable, that mouth. Somehow he knew it. But she wore a respirator. And angels would not need respirators, even here on Mars.

"Did I . . . lose the leg?" he mumbled.

She jerked, stared down at him, then turned her head away to call to someone he could not see. The name she called was Karl.

A tall, youngish-looking man in a travel-stained thermalsuit came to look down at M'Cord over the girl's shoulder. He had the soft, silken, white-blond hair and transparent white skin of some Scandinavians, especially Swedes. His face was tired and his blue eyes—weary, and very like the girl's—had fear in them. He cleared his throat awkwardly.

"How do you feel, Cn. M'Cord?" he asked in a high, husky voice.

"Empty . . . washed out," said M'Cord. "You a doctor?"

The blond man shook his head. "Archaeologist. But Inga trained as a medic, once."

"Inga?" M'Cord cocked an eyebrow at the girl. "Your wife?"

For some reason, the blond man flushed scarlet.

"My sister. Excuse me, Citizen. My name is Nordgren, Dr. Karl Nordgren. Formerly of the Stockholm Institute of Extraterrestrial Historical Studies. Now on sabbatical, attached to the Syrtis Colonial Administration Department of Cultural Affairs."

M'Cord digested this slowly. He grunted: "You already know my name. How did you—"

Nordgren cleared his throat again; it was a habit with him.

"We've been here two weeks. Came here from Syrtis across the Aeria dustlands as part of a motorized caravan

72

bound for Sigeus Portus. The caravan was sent out by the Administration as part of a geological survey of the Sinus. As you probably know, preliminary surveys have indicated that the Sabaeus Sinus Plateau is possibly the oldest, continually-exposed land-surface on Mars. It was above water even when there were oceans here, millions of years ago. It has probably been surface land as far back as there was surface land—since the planet was formed, in other words. Well, not to digress further: we parted company with the geologists at Sigeus and came here by *slidar* with native bearers. I—we—wished to check firsthand the rumors that laid the site of the legendary 'first city,' Ygnarh, somewhere in this region." His lips twisted ironically, and he wet them with the tip of his tongue.

"And what happened?"

Nordgren shrugged. "As soon as our bearers got wind of what we were looking for, they deserted en masse. We were lucky to get here at all; they did leave us two *slidars* and some of the supplies. We found Ygnarh, all right; or a very ancient city, at any rate. One not previously known. But then the—the outlaws came. And since then we have been prisoners, as you and your friends are."

"So it wasn't a dream then? Chastar and the girl and the other man—?"

"The renegade priest? No; they're very real, I'm afraid."

The girl, who had knelt by his cot all this while, with her eyes lowered while her brother spoke in his high-pitched, nervous voice, now stirred fretfully.

"He should rest, Karl."

Nordgren blinked. "Of course—stupid of me. There will be time to talk later, I am sure." He faded into the background; M'Cord never saw him go. Things were getting hazy. He felt sleep welling up about him, like warm, soft waters.

"Did I . . . lose the leg?" he asked again, drowsily.

73

She shook her head, cornsilk curls tousling. "We saved it. One of the things the bearers left behind when they deserted us was a new Atwood M-400. I had a store of power cells in my kit, which they didn't bother with—you probably know how they fear our devil-magic. . . ."

"Atwood?" he murmured sleepily.

She nodded. "One of those new 'marvels of electronic medicine,' as the newscasters call it. Accelerates the regrowth and repair of bone and tissue by direct electronic stimulation of the cellular . . ."

But her voice faded out as darkness closed around him. And he slept. But this time it was a deep, restful, healing sleep, unshadowed by memories of pain. And when he woke he felt fit again.

Over the next couple of days—M'Cord was never too certain of the lapse of time spent in Ygnarh—he had many opportunities to talk with the Swedish girl and her brother. They were an odd pair, he thought. He sensed something peculiar between them, without ever quite knowing what it was. He had too many other things to worry about to bother puzzling his head over their secret, whatever it was.

Among the other things he learned by listening to the Nordgrens talk was the reason why he and Thaklar still lived. For Chastar would have slain them long ago, even without Zerild's insistence, had it not been for the recalcitrance of the Dragon Hawk.

Thaklar, it seemed, refused to divulge the secret of the missing empty place on the map unless he was permitted to accompany the outlaws on the road to the mysterious Valley.

And he would not go without M'Cord.

The snake-eyed little renegade priest whispered of ways to make even the strongest and bravest of men talk freely, whether he wanted to or not. Chastar was probably tempted—he hated Thaklar, if only because he suspected there was more between the warrior prince and the dancing girl than either of them would admit. But even the red wolf knew that torture would not do the trick. The Hawk warriors never yielded under torment; they would die, however slowly, with closed mouths. And there was another reason: they could not trust Thaklar not to take his final, secret revenge. That is, whatever they pried from his stubborn lips under the persuasion of red-hot knives—might not be correct. If there were man traps along the way, as was probably the case, Thaklar might well tell them wrong, dying with the comforting knowledge that his tormentors would not long outlive him.

No, even the hasty-tempered and murderous wolf knew that the best way—the only way, really—was to take Thaklar with them, riding in front, so that if he meant to betray them to their deaths, he himself would be the first to die.

But before he would accompany them, M'Cord must be healed and fit. Chastar swore and fumed, but there was nothing else to do but wait while the big Earthman mended slowly under the medicine of the blond girl.

Actually, he mended more swiftly than seemed possible. This was due in a large measure to the highly sophisticated medical equipment the Nordgrens had brought on their expedition. And it was also due to the simple fact that on Mars an Earthman gets no infection from a wound. The two races, whether originally one in the dawn of time, as some theories hinted, had at least evolved in total isolation from each other over millions of years. Martian bacteria found it difficult to flourish in the different body chemistry of Earthmen. Not impossible, for there were some diseases which were virulent enough to be shared by the two branches of humanity: but difficult.

In M'Cord's case, it was not so much ordinary infection that had attacked the wound and driven him into the red madness of fever, as it was the venom of the sandcat. Unlike terrene predators, the few dangerous beasts who still dwell in the Martian wastelands carry their venom in sacs at the base of their claws, which are hollow, as are the fangs of vipers.

Sandcat poison attacks the blood cells of both Earthman and native Martian. It was that that had poisoned M'Cord, almost to the edge of death.

But when nature hurts, she also heals. And in the very body of the sandcat she long ago hid the means of counteracting its venom. For a tiny parasite that infests the spinal scales of the predator contains a pharmaceutical that nullifies the poison in its claws. From the bodies of these parasites Earthside chemists had long ago learned to prepare an antitoxin that negated the effects of sandcat venom with magical swiftness. The serum was rare and expensive, which was why M'Cord had carried none with him.

The other factor that hastened his return to health was his strength and toughness, endurance and vitality. M'Cord had lived in the dustlands, sometimes for a year at a time. A man may go into that dry hell soft and weak, but if he comes out of it alive, he comes out lean and sinewy and strong. The fat and softness are burned out of a man in the fierce, cold crucible of the desert. And M'Cord was all leather and steel wire inside; there was no weakness in him.

And so he healed—slowly—and in time became whole again. There were drugs to control the pain and drugs to fight the infection and drugs to clear the mind and drugs to knit the torn flesh and frayed muscle. M'Cord wished, sourly, that there were drugs in the pharmacopoeia to erase memories. And perhaps there were.

Thaklar was stiff and formal and silent, keeping a closed face and hooded eyes before the others. Only M'Cord sensed the depth of pain in the Dragon Hawk prince who had become his brother; and only M'Cord felt that he was planning something. Revenge? What else could it be but revenge—revenge against the woman who had wronged him so cruelly?

They were hardly ever together, Thaklar and the big Earthman he had carried in his arms across the dustlands. Always they were watched, either by the cool, amused eyes of Zerild or by the flat, reptilian gaze of Phuun. So there was no chance for M'Cord to ask what his brother planned to do.

Indeed, there wasn't much they could do—unless the hawk-faced warrior had an ace up his sleeve, which M'Cord doubted. They had been thoroughly disarmed and their baggage searched for weapons. With M'Cord half crippled, they could not possibly hope to take the three by surprise and overcome them hand to hand. And all three of the outlaws wore weapons night and day.

And, to make things even more difficult, Chastar certainly suspected the Hawk of scheming something of the sort. He was tense and wary and nervous as a cat, and he never relaxed. At night they slept apart, M'Cord on his cot in the room next to the two Swedes, in a room with no windows, whose door could be barred from the outside. Thaklar bedded down in a small cubicle off the main rotunda, a strong-walled little room, equally windowless, and with a heavy door that could also be barred. To make things worse, the little renegade priestling curled up in his bedroll before the threshold so their break for freedom would not come by night.

M'Cord began to wonder if it would come at all. He wished he could read his brother's mind. He half expected Thaklar to slip him a note sometime when they ate together or worked together with the pressure-still, condensing the day's ration of water from the blue, thick-leafed, rubbery plants. But never a note was passed in this way,

77

and never came the opportunity to exchange even a few words together in private, for they were never left alone.

Finally M'Cord shrugged and gave up wondering. When it came, it would come—if it was ever to come!

He settled down to the slow process of rebuilding his torn body and his drained, exhausted strength.

IX. A City Like a Skull

Just waiting to mend, he discovered, was worse than just waiting for something—anything—to happen. The tensions in the camp were like coiled springs, or a charge of ionite with a slow-trigger fuse. The explosion was bound to come sooner or later; and when it came, M'Cord wanted to be on his feet and ready to do his bit.

But getting back on his feet was not all that easy, he found, even with the new wonders of electronic medicine. The claws of the sandcat had torn him viciously, and muscle tissue is the hardest of all to heal.

He had lost an awful lot of blood in the dustlands before Thaklar had managed to close his wound. The blood loss had drained his vitality, weakened him dreadfully; and the fever and the infection or poisoning or whatever it was had not helped.

Blood plasma, of course, was no longer used—had not been much in use for the better part of a century. Dexyrine-20 had taken its place: a pharmaceutical that worked directly on the body's ability to generate new blood cells. It was a small, grim irony that M'Cord had packed no dexyrine-20 in his medikit when getting ready to leave

Sun Lake City. But the Nordgrens had the stuff, and finally he began to mend.

"Plenty of rest and sleep and good food," Nordgren reiterated solemnly, "are better for you than all the medicines." M'Cord grunted sourly, but submitted to the regimen. He had to admit that he was feeling better all the time.

He saw little of Nordgren, save in the evenings, when they all huddled together in a large room of the ruined palace. It was there that the outlaws had installed their heat unit. Without the unit the Earthsiders might well have frozen to death, for nights were cold and bitter in the deep canyons of the plateau.

By day, Nordgren insisted on continuing with his work. Chastar, who had long ago summed up the tall, nervous, blond man and had dismissed him as a harmless weakling, let him go about the city to perform his devil-magic, which was incomprehensible to the Martians. So he mapped the dead husk of a city and photographed its monuments with an expensive depth camera never intended for desert use and took rubbings of a few shallow and time-worn reliefs.

Chastar understood none of this, which deepened his contempt for the scientist, since the outlaw was the sort of man who tended to sneer at and feel disgust for anything he couldn't understand—but which another man could. The Martians, as a race, had little interest in their own past, M'Cord knew. Just living, managing to stay alive from day to day and struggling to eke out a meager living from their dead dustball of a planet, was a matter which consumed their every waking moment—fussing over the glories of the past and preserving their ancient monuments was a luxury they could hardly afford.

So, what with one thing and another, M'Cord spent most of his waking hours in the company of the girl, Inga. He hardly thought of her as a woman, although she was young and would have been beautiful were it not for the weariness and strain in her face and the strange shadow that haunted her eyes. They talked little.

When he had regained his strength and began to feel well again, and able to hobble about stiffly for a little while each day, the girl led him out into the courtyard, where he could get some sun.

The old palace in which they camped was rude and simple and small, by High Martian standards. There were no tessellated floors or wall murals or delicately carved architraves or capitals, such as he had seen in other native ruins. He could well believe the city was as old as the legends said it was.

He basked in the sun, trying to ignore the stiffness in his lame leg, and let the girl talk. She had a nervous habit of expounding on any subject that made her sound like her brother. M'Cord wondered lazily if she had acquired the habit out of admiration for him, in an attempt to be more like him, or whether it was simply that when she talked she did not have to think about whatever it was that was eating at her. For something was eating at her, he knew; and something gnawed within Karl Nordgren, too. It was as if the two of them shared a guilty secret that bound them together.

One day in particular she talked about the city itself. The sun hung low in the west and the purple shadows of evening were thickening in deep pools of gloom beneath the broken walls. As the light dimmed it became more difficult to see the marks of age and decay. In the dimming light it was almost as if the old city still lived and was not just a worn and hollowed skull of a city. You could ignore the desert dust wind-drifted into every corner. You could overlook the columns that lay fallen and shattered on the uneven and broken pave. The rich, soft light made glowing and glamorous the carved stone and made it seem young again, as a heavy coating of cosmetic restores the

81

illusion of vanished youthfulness to the withered cheeks of an aged queen.

The girl stood staring dreamily across the central plaza, where the fronts of ancient palaces stood, seemingly whole again. Something of her wistful mood was communicated to M'Cord: one could almost have thought that in the next moment the lordly princes of Old Mars would come striding grandly out of the shadows to stroll and intrigue and converse in the twilight. If ever a dead city had ghosts, thought M'Cord, it was Ygnarh dreaming of her lost empire in the golden twilight. . . .

The girl shivered suddenly, as if touched by his thought.

"Cold? Maybe we should go in."

She shook her head. "In a moment. I was just thinking . . . how beautiful it all is."

"It is that," he grunted, shifting weight from his game leg, which stiffened and ached sometimes in the cold of nightfall. "Is it really so old as the legends tell?"

She shrugged. "Older, probably. It was already old before the first of our ancestors learned to walk upright and to clench a sharp stone in his fist for a weapon. It was empty and abandoned before even the Martian history began, much less our own."

"It really is Ygnarh, then?" he asked. M'Cord had been on Mars long enough to know how easily legends grow, and how little there is to most of them. The girl shrugged again.

"Ygnarh simply means 'the old city.' The oldest, or the earliest, which the Martians themselves remembered or had any record of. The legends barely whisper of it; it was here in Ygnarh that Zoram became Prince of the Children of Yhoom . . . the first clan, you know . . . the first king . . . long before Thomra welded the ten nations into one and set himself over all of the People as their first Jamad Tengru."

82

"But is this Ygnarh itself, the actual place?" he persisted.

"Karl says it's hard to be certain there was ever just one city that was known as Ygnarh. We haven't found the name of this city in any of the inscriptions, so we can't know for sure what the folk who lived here called it."

"There *are* inscriptions, then? I haven't seen any."

"There are a few; mostly on the ancestral tablets in the round citadel by the ruined aqueduct. Karl says that it is either a temple *per se* or an early House of Ancestors. Actually, we haven't found anything that looks like a regular temple yet. Karl says he thinks the people who lived here were too familiar with their gods to be in awe of them yet, or to worship them . . . any more than Adam, fresh-come from Eden, bothered with the building of churches. The inscriptions are very difficult to make any sense of, being in the earliest known form of the pictographs; we have only an imperfect knowledge of them, even now."

She shivered again.

"You sure you aren't getting cold?" he asked.

"No . . . it's not that."

"Well, what is it then? Ghosts of the past?"

She smiled faintly. "Something like that, I guess. It's the . . . how very *old* it is! Look at this stone."

She indicated the plinth of a column. It was of the pale-golden, clear marble the High Martians had used in their architecture. It wasn't the same stone, geologically, that they called marble back on Earth, but it resembled it in its sleek, glistening polish, and in the way veins of some glinting, quartz-like mineral threaded through it, and in its density and hardness. But, unlike marble as it was known back on Earth, this stone had the clear lucency of alabaster. But it endured the weathering and wear of ages like no form of alabaster could; once buffed to a high gloss, it held its slick polish for ages.

"See how worn the stone is, how it crumbles?" she murmured, running her palm over the plinth. He touched it curiously: the surface of the golden marble was powdery, scored with a million tiny cracks and flaws. No vandal's ax had hacked it into wreckage; the slow erosion of immeasurable time had worn away the stone, grain by grain. He nodded.

"Imagine how long it would take the stone to wear to this condition," she said softly. "You know how durable this marble is . . . imagine the aeons it took to wear the stone away like this . . . on a planet where there has been neither rain nor frost nor snow nor hurricane for a million years or more."

Now it was he who shivered a little, at the thought. It was as if the impalpable weight of all those ages settled upon him, cold and soft as the very shadows. *This stone was already old and worn before Babylon was a village,* he thought, *before the first pyramid was raised, or the first man learned to write.*

Almost as if she heard the echo of his thought, the girl whispered: "They set this stone here before the glaciers came down across Europe. And it was hewn out of the hills before our first ancestor walked upright. . . ."

The mood stretched between them, something deep and uncanny; something which they shared between them. He had almost reached out to touch her—

"Inga?" a high, nervous voice spoke from the gloom of the arcade.

She started, and turned away. The mood broke, jarringly. And the moment was gone before it could be acted upon.

"Here, Karl!"

"What are you thinking of?" her brother demanded querulously, stepping out of the shadows to blink owlishly at them through his glasses. "It is nearly dark, and Cn.

84

M'Cord should be inside, out of the cold. You know how the cold stiffens his leg."

She flushed and dropped her eyes, absurdly like a little girl being scolded.

"Yes, Karl . . . I'm sorry, Karl . . . we were only . . ."

"Never mind! Come inside, now. Help Cn. M'Cord—see, his leg has stiffened already. How thoughtless of you, Inga! We will talk later."

The girl, head bent, shuffled within, and Nordgren helped the lame man to his feet. Something about the touch of his hands—cold and dry and, somehow, reptilian—sent a shudder of revulsion through M'Cord. Just as something in the girl's frightened, submissive voice knotted his stomach with a qualm of disgust he could not quite explain. He sensed something here, something between these two, something buried and hidden away but hideously close to the surface and hideously alive.

And it was something he did not like.

He went in to dinner.

Every day or two, Chastar rode off down the ravine to hunt for meat. The Earthsiders had canned rations and the Martians had their tough, dried, preserved meats, but these were to be reserved for emergencies. Chastar liked to prove his manhood in the hunt, it seemed. Or perhaps he simply enjoyed killing something. At any rate, he was an efficient hunter and knew how to find the cave reptiles and the rock lizards, which afforded them a plentiful supply of succulent meat, which Inga cooked into a delicious stew, using precious water from the still to moisten the meal.

Chastar would come cantering back into camp with scarlet or golden game slung across the withers of his steed, hallooing and roaring with high zestful good humor. Nursing an ache in his cramped muscles, M'Cord more than

85

once wished the swaggering huntsman would fall off his loper and break his neck. But this never happened, unfortunately.

At night he lay in his thermosac, staring up at the roof, waiting for the pain to subside beneath the smothering numbness of the drugs. Waiting for Thaklar to make his move—or for Zerild to put a knife between Chastar's ribs —was beginning to get on his nerves.

He wished it were all over. But he knew it would be a long time before it was.

X. A Time of Waiting

And so he slept and ate and exercised and rested, and took his medicines as Inga Nordgren directed. But he watched and listened all the time. And his mind was ever busy.

There would be a strange group, they who were to search for the Valley.

There was Chastar, for one. He was easy enough to figure out. A criminal, fled from the justice of his kind, an ordinary outlaw. Ever suspicious, ever wary, with murder in his wolfish eyes and a gun never far from his side. He hated all men because he could not trust them, believing that they were as treacherous and unscrupulous as he was.

A man like that, M'Cord knew, lives on his image of himself, a bundle of naked and raw nerve endings—easily angered, easily driven to kill. And his image was that of the rampant male, all swagger and bluster. To fulfill his image of himself, he needed a woman—any woman— every woman. His sense of manhood was not complete without sexual conquest.

He found such a woman in Zerild. She herself was his very counterpart—free as the wind, savage as the desert, deadly as truth. Quick to kill and even quicker to betray. The eternal temptress and betrayer: the taunting witch-woman, all Lilith and Salome and Delilah, with no bit of Eve within her.

Being so very like Chastar, she denied him the gift of herself. Being Chastar, that denial frayed him to the quick and nagged him raw. He would more easily have killed her than ever he could let her go untouched. But Zerild, being Zerild, would have slain any man who took her by force. And in her own way she was every bit as deadly and dangerous as he.

So they lived side by side—unlovers. She flaunted before him the temptation of her body, and he strove ever to win it. The tension between them was savage. Some-day, thought M'Cord, it would snap and there would be red murder between them and one or the other or possibly both would never see another dawn. He wryly hoped he would not be around to see the outcome.

The renegade priest was quite another breed. Some-where, somehow, he had betrayed his vows and had been defrocked—if that was the word. The little old man was as closemouthed as they come, and kept to himself as much as he dared. Toward the girl Zerild he maintained a guarded silence, seldom speaking to her, never responding to her taunts when she lashed out at whoever was nearest, which was very often. Only the dull fire that glittered be-hind his slitted eyes showed that he heard the words she flung at him. Words like "eunuch" and "worm."

Toward Chastar he groveled in the most obsequious and servile manner, bearing himself humbly, calling the outlaw "master" and "lord," and enduring his curses and careless buffets with silence. He *endured,* did Phuun. It was as if he waited for some high moment to come when he could revenge himself magnificently and finally for all the words of slighting and contempt.

Of the three, M'Cord thought Phuun the most deadly.

He made certain never to turn his back upon the renegade priestling, and never to be alone with him.

So, bit by bit, he began to mend; and when he was feeling fit once more, and could hobble about a little, he sought the sunshine and the open air. Cooped up in the darkness was never M'Cord's way; and besides, one learns nothing when one is tucked out of sight in a corner.

Sprawled lazily, napping in the sun, he kept his eyes and ears open. Except for the Nordgrens and Thaklar, none of the others had visited him during his recovery. He wanted to see them firsthand, and study them himself.

They were a weirdly mixed trio—the wolf-like outlaw, the witch-girl, and the viper-like little ex-priest. M'Cord could not help wondering what had brought them together in the first place. And there was also another thing to wonder about.

Why did they seek The Holy?

It was not out of piety, that was certain. For one thing, the gods had long ago forbidden the Valley to men; just as, long ago and on another world, a certain Garden had been made forever inaccessible to the descendants of a man called Adam. And for much the same reason. But more to the point, none of the three gave any credence to the ancient faith of their kind. No, there was another motive. . . .

There was mention of treasure. Treasure, to such as Chastar, meant gold or gems. But all of the accounts of the Valley Where Life Was Born that M'Cord could remember (and he dredged up from the depths of his memory every tiniest scrap of legend and lore concerning the place that he had ever come across in all his years on Mars) described a paradisical garden with a pool. Nary a word of gold or gems. What, then, was the treasure?

Perhaps it was immortality itself. Treasure enough to a sick or dying man—especially a rich one, who could afford to pay splendidly for immortal youth. But M'Cord suspected there was something more to it than that. That was too simple—too obvious.

And it did not explain the cunning in the priest's eyes when he talked of the days to come, nor the greed that lay naked in the gloating, hungry eyes of Chastar when he listened.

Well, whatever their scheme, it would come to light in time. As ever, thought M'Cord, time would tell. . . .

Of course, he had no way of guessing how strange and awful the secret would be, when all was finally laid bare in the end.

But that is one of the best things about living—one of the most precious gifts ever given to us by Those who shaped our being: We cannot ever know what is to come.

He slept and rested, took his meals and his medicines, and lazed in the open sun, feeling the strength seep back bit by bit into his battered body.

He watched and waited; listened and observed.

The strains and tensions between this odd, mixed bag of treasure seekers was like a textbook in human relations gone sick and sour. He didn't completely understand all of the emotions he observed around him, but he caught enough of them.

The key figure, oddly enough, seemed to be Thaklar.

It was Thaklar who held the secret of Ophar the Holy— only he could guide them through the empty place on the old silver chart. M'Cord wondered if he intended to do so. It was impossible to tell. Thaklar was closely watched at all times, and he kept his own counsels. Even when he was with the others, he seemed to be alone with his thoughts, ignoring their spats and quarrels.

M'Cord noticed that the Hawk warrior kept to himself as much as he possibly could. He maintained a calm mien of self-control whenever Chastar burst into one of his snarling, spitting rages of frustration and fury. He did not grovel, nor did he fight. Generally, he laughed. He knew how to handle men like the wolf, did Thaklar. The world was full of them.

Toward Zerild, Thaklar turned deaf ears and blind eyes. He made utterly no response, either to her flaunting or her contempt. He behaved as though she were not there. It was that, as much as anything, that stung the girl. In order to sustain her belief that men were worthy of nothing but her fierce contempt, they had to behave contemptuously toward her. They had to lust for her tawny loveliness, which she dangled ever just beyond their reach. Or they had to flinch beneath her stinging tongue, and hate her.

Thaklar did neither. He ignored the temptation she offered, as he ignored her mockery. Once burned, twice shy, M'Cord thought with amusement.

He himself did not even pretend to ignore her. When she came swaggering about, mischief glinting in the sidelong glances she flicked in his direction, he responded openly with an admiration undisguised, although colored with amusement. He kept himself out of reach of her claws, and he made himself immune to her taunts by pretending to be amused. He acted like an indulgent uncle who notices, but does not really believe in, the flirting ways of a small niece.

She knew that game as well, of course, and they played it often. But she was not really concerned with M'Cord, so she did not really bother trying to make him love or desire her. It was a reflex, little more. She could no more pass by anything male without flaunting herself before it than she could fly. They played the game, but their hearts were not really in it.

As for the brother and sister, they were mostly ignored. Chastar regarded them as a mere annoyance, something to be brushed aside and swatted bloodily, as you swat a fly when it bothers you. They were alive still because they had been needed to heal M'Cord. And he had not killed them before Thaklar and M'Cord had arrived, largely because it was difficult for Chastar to make up his mind to do anything. He was too tightly strung, too filled with trembling rage and fury, to think or plan coolly. That was Zerild's job, to think and to plan.

Chastar was all wild, nervous impulse. He knew where he wanted to be but could never plot or scheme in order to get there. So he struck out blindly, hating himself and everything else. He had not slain the Nordgrens before because he had not been able to make up his mind to do so; and afterward, he had not been able to kill them because he needed them.

Now that they were no longer needed, M'Cord was afraid that Chastar would kill them out of hand. He didn't want that to happen. There was no particular reason for it to which he could put a name. He didn't much like Nordgren—the nervous, awkward, impractical man was all brain, no blood. All talk and theory, no action. But he didn't want him killed; after all, he owed him and the girl something for healing his leg. But M'Cord was a hard, practical man, and a realist. He put little value on any life but his own, and not too high a value on that.

He wished he knew what was in Thaklar's mind. He wished he had some idea of what the Hawk warrior was planning—if, indeed, he was planning anything. Maybe he was just drifting with the tide, was Thaklar. Waiting for an opening to strike, waiting for a rotten spot to turn up so that he could use the soft place to his advantage. But they were seldom allowed to be together, and were never together without being observed. Usually it was the priestling, Phuun, who was sent along to watch and listen when they talked. Sometimes it was the girl. Never once were they by themselves so that M'Cord could ask Thaklar what he planned to do.

He gave up wondering about it, and just lived from day to day, regaining his strength as swiftly as he could.

The leg healed, but it would never be the same again. The muscles were badly torn and, while they had knitted, after a fashion, they would never be strong again. M'Cord would be a cripple for the rest of his life, dragging behind him the dead weight of one half-alive leg, an object of contempt and derision.

It made him bitter and even cynical to think about it— he who had been bitter and cynical enough without this added reason. He felt himself less than a full man, with the leg. What woman would look on him as anything more than a cripple, deserving of pity?

He hated the leg. Which meant he hated himself. Always he had prided himself on his body, on its strength and toughness. Now it betrayed him with its weakness. His life was ended, he thought blackly in the empty hours of the night when he lay awake, waiting for dawn. A man with a dead leg could not fend for himself in the dustlands, could not prospect for power-metal in the plateaux. How would he end up, as a filthy wino sleeping in the back alleys of Sun Lake City, begging for a coin?

It was an ugly thing to think about. Maybe it would have been better if he had died there in the dustlands of the Regio, under the claws of the sandcat. . . .

But there was a core of toughness left even in his fever-worn and crippled body. M'Cord was still alive, and was regaining his strength day by day. He would live as long as he could, he thought; and he would come out of this as best he might.

Meanwhile, there was nothing to do but sweat it out and hope that Chastar didn't kill them all in a sudden spasm of wild, maniacal fury.

Somewhere along the way to Ophar it would happen— whatever was going to happen.

Or in Ophar itself.

That thought made him smile grimly to himself, there in the dark as he lay sleeplessly staring into blackness and waiting for the drugs to take hold.

Who could say what would happen?

And—who knew?—maybe there really *was* treasure to be found in the Valley Beyond Time.

XI. They Leave Ygnarh

M'Cord healed. He could walk about the plaza well enough, dragging the half-dead leg behind him. He could even climb fairly well. And—with Chastar watching him with a rifle ready in his hands in case the *F'yagh* should try to make a break for freedom—he found he could sit a saddle again without any particular discomfort.

"Then why do we linger here in the city-of-ghosts, master?" that little priestling hissed in that snakish way he had which made M'Cord's hackles rise. "The treasure of all the world waits out there at the end of the Road. If the accursed ones are to go with us to The Holy, well then, let us be gone."

Chastar growled and spat. "We go when I say so, snake —not one moment before!" Then, turning his hot eyes on Inga, the outlaw demanded, "Is he truly well enough to ride then, yellow-hair?" Inga said, in her calm way, that M'Cord was. His eyes ran over her, slowly, his glance lingering on her full, ripe breasts. She endured the touch of his eyes in silence, although M'Cord, watching from the corner, knotted his fists and held his breath. The outlaw had never touched Inga, as far as he knew, being preoccupied with the witch-girl, Zerild. But there was a first time for everything.

But then Zerild said something caustic and humorous: the mood broke abruptly, and Chastar laughed in his spitting, snarling way. And M'Cord slowly uncurled his fists and let the moment pass without comment.

The girl, Inga, seemed unconcerned, as if she had noticed nothing. And perhaps, after all, she had not felt the pressure of those hungry eyes feeling and tasting her body. She was still something of an enigma to M'Cord. She could have been beautiful, he thought; her body was ripe and desirable under the loose folds of the baggy thermal-suit. But she did nothing with herself to catch the eyes of men.

It was not a question of cosmetics or hairdos, of course, for these were not to be had in the dustlands beyond the handful of Earthsider colonies. Zerild herself did not bother to paint her lips or eyes, and tied her hair carelessly back out of the way with a twist of scarlet cloth. What it was, then, was that the young woman maintained a placidity that was unappetizing. She hardly ever met his eye—any eye—squarely and frankly; her head seemed ever bent, as if she went always bowed down by some invisible weight of guilt or sin or worry.

She never laughed, or sang, or seemed happy. Always she seemed to be working. When she was not cleaning or cooking or tending M'Cord, she was busy copying her brother's notes or filing his depth photos and tomb-rubbings; she always busied herself with something.

He decided it was not so much her cow-like calm, her yielding before any demand or pressure without complaint, that bugged him. It was the strain and tiredness he sensed within her that irritated him and made her seem less than a young woman and more like some listless squaw, broken in spirit, robbed of the freshness and luster of her youthfulness, made old and tired before her time. There was a slack fatigue visible in her face that kept it from seeming vivid and sparkling—a dull heaviness to her eyes. Perhaps she would never be truly beautiful, even under the best of conditions—the angel-vision he had seemed to see bending over him that first time he had awakened from his pain-shot stupor, he had long ago dismissed as an illusion of vivid youth and beauty—but if she had laughed a little, and let the light come into her eyes, she would have seemed attractive.

But she did not.

He wondered, what had robbed her of her youth; and what weird and unholy shadow hung over her, blighting and withering her charm.

Well, there were a lot of things he would never know; most likely, this was only one of them.

Finally Chastar made up his mind. The blustering bully seemed to find it difficult to control his temper and his nervous energy long enough to arrive at any decision. But he abruptly stated one afternoon that since all was ready, it was time to depart. On the morrow they would saddle up and ride out of the dead city and seek the Valley Where Life Was Born.

There was an uncanny glitter in his eyes as he gave the command. And a look passed between him and the gaunt, hunched old priest, whom M'Cord neither understood nor liked. He would like very much to have known just what it was they hoped to find in the fabulous Valley. Well, soon enough, he would know!

So the time had come at last for the adventure to begin. They no longer had any reason to remain in the ruins of Ygnarh. M'Cord was as healed as he would ever be; if he could walk none too well, at least he could ride without pain. And now Chastar fretted to be off.

The Nordgrens were to accompany them, after all. The decision had been Chastar's alone, and it came as a surprise. M'Cord decided that the canny outlaw must have felt that the more hostages to fortune he could bring, the better. Chastar still suspected Thaklar of leading them into some kind of a trap. And while he knew that Thaklar had no particular reason to place any value on the lives of the two Earthsiders, at least they could be forced to ride in the fore, so that if any traps were to be sprung, it would be Karl and Inga Nordgren who would suffer, and not he or Phuun or Zerild.

And after them would ride M'Cord. He was saving M'Cord because he knew very well that Thaklar prized the life of the Hated One he called his brother. Thaklar would do much to keep M'Cord from harm, the outlaw knew. M'Cord was the best hostage of all.

So they packed their gear—the Nordgrens bundling up their possessions under the fierce, suspicious eye of Chastar himself, who was wary of *F'yagha* magic—and loaded the pack-beasts with food and blankets and waterskins. The Nordgrens had their own pressure-still, and the outlaws another; the one M'Cord had been using on his prospecting trip had broken down in the Regio. But there would be enough for all to eat and drink, and the beasts as well.

"It is criminal to require me to abandon all my records and notes!" Nordgren protested to M'Cord as they saddled the *slidars*. "Why can they not simply leave us here, as they found us? I have no interest in this treasure of theirs, this sacred Valley, which is only a myth anyway! I have my work to do; and what we have discovered here is of immense importance to science! The oldest city on Mars—perhaps even the very first city, if the legends are true—oh, why can't they leave Inga and me here to do our work in peace?"

98

"Be glad you've still got a whole skin," M'Cord growled under his breath. "If Chastar didn't need us to test the way for deadfalls and man traps, he'd as lief slit our throats and leave us all here. Think of your sister, man, and forget about your notes."

"But all my work . . ." Nordgren protested feebly. Then he caught the fierce, hard glint in M'Cord's eye and wilted.

"Inga, of course . . . yes, there's Inga. But the notes and the photographs . . ."

M'Cord said nothing further, but his lips tightened a little. Like most hard men who lived under the harsh law of survive-or-die, there was little room in him for the softer sentiments. But he had a rough chivalry of his own and it galled him to listen to this vapid fool babbling about his precious bits of paper, and holding them more valuable than the girl who stood at his side, silently strapping the saddle on her beast without asking for help or even complaining.

He knew she had overheard them, for her face was carefully blank and her eyes, when he caught a glimpse of them, were dull and empty. For a moment or two he wondered why a young and handsome woman had bound herself into servitude to her brother's career, rather than making one of her own, or getting a husband and a family.

Then he shrugged and climbed into the saddle. It was none of his business, after all.

They rode out of Ygnarh, the three Earthsiders leading, the outlaws riding behind, with Thaklar between them. Nordgren continued to fuss and fret, mumbling under his breath until M'Cord, whose leg was hurting him a little, growled at him.

"For God's sake, man, stop whining and whimpering like a child deprived of his favorite toys! Your stuff will be safe—didn't we bundle it up in airtight plasticine so nothing could damage it?—it will still be here when we get back, won't it?"

"Yes, of course, you're right. I really shouldn't fret so, but how do we know we ever *will* get back, after all?" the other man pursued the point, querulously. "I mean, we don't even know where we're going, do we—actually? The native literature is filled with legends of lost cities and fabulous treasure-troves, but only seldom is there anything to substantiate them . . ."

He cantered ahead of them a bit, still complaining to himself. M'Cord fell back to ride with Inga. She sat stiffly in the saddle, staring straight ahead, her eyes heavy, her face expressionless under the respirator which masked her nose and mouth.

"I . . . I'm sorry," he said gruffly.

"Don't be sorry, Cn. M'Cord," she said tonelessly. "I don't mind; really I don't. Karl's work always comes first . . . it really is *very* important, you know."

There was nothing else to say, so he said nothing. But he was thinking about where they were going, and wondering if they would get there.

By this time they had all seen the map. Chastar had forced Zerild to show it openly. It was a thin plate of worn old silver, engraved with a pattern of delicate lines. As Thaklar had claimed, a portion of it was smooth and blank. That was the portion that lay at the end of the Road, just before they supposedly were to enter the mystic Valley where the Pool of Life waited to be found. But there would be many days of riding before they reached that point.

Comparing the old silver plate to CA survey charts he had seen, M'Cord realized that if the Valley existed at all, which was probably the case, it was deep in the very center of a region the Earthmen knew as Meridiani Sinus, which lay due west of the Sabaeus. In fact, it occurred to him to wonder if the place they were headed for might not be a small crater in the middle of the Meridiani the Earthmen called Airy, for some obscure reason. If his hunch proved correct, it would be a rather amusing coincidence. Because it was that particular crater, a small and unimportant one, that the mapmakers back on Earth had chosen to mark the position of the prime meridian—the Martian Greenwich, they called it.

It would certainly be an odd coincidence. . . .

So they rode out of the gates of age-old Ygnarh one chilly dawn and M'Cord went with them. He kept his eyes on Thaklar as best he could, waiting for a sign.

Whenever the signal came, he planned to be ready.

At last they were on the move, he thought with dour satisfaction. Any change in the intolerable tensions that had grown between them from being cooped up together all this while would be a change for the better.

However, it was not exactly the most pleasant trip he could imagine, nor the easiest.

They were already in the least known, least explored part of the ancient planet. Here, at least, they were safe. But now they were setting out into the unknown . . . with a million-year-old map to guide them . . . bound for a forgotten paradise of the gods, which had been forbidden to man since the beginnings of human life on this planet.

Their leader was a ravenous wolf—a madman, a killer. And by his side went a sullen renegade priest who was no less mad; and a witch-girl who betrayed friend and comrade and lover alike, for her own zest and pleasure.

And ahead of them lay a mystery that had been hidden from the dawn of time. They would be the first to trespass upon its secrets.

He only hoped they would not awaken whatever forgotten gods or ghosts or devils had slept there undisturbed down the dim corridors of immeasurable ages.

XII. The Road

So they rode out of the gates of elder Ygnarh one morning quite early when the black-purple night sky had barely paled with dawn to the color of dark slate, under a dim and wintry sun.

The city was built in a wide, circular depression in the plateau, which was hundreds of feet below the surface of the tableland. When the seas had dried up, the continental land-surfaces had cracked and split apart and were cloven by deep gorges and ravines, too many to be explored in a thousand years, too many even to be mapped.

But the worn old map on the plate of ancient silver showed the way.

All that first day they followed one particular gorge that zigzagged deep into the center of the plateau. Toward nightfall they came to an abrupt turning point which was clearly indicated on the chart, which was their guide. From here they must ascend to the upper surface of the tableland, but this proved not to be very difficult, for the strata had worn away over the ages into a series of stone steps like a staircase built by giants, and the *slidars* could climb as well as any man.

The first night they made camp in a bowl-shaped depression atop the plateau, under the blaze of the naked stars. Nordgren thought it likely that the bowl was a very ancient impact crater. All this equatorial region of Mars had been peppered by meteorites since the time, long ago, when the oxygen-rich atmosphere of the youthful planet had begun to thin. The crater was so worn that it could have been a million years old, he theorized; perhaps more. M'Cord couldn't have cared less. His leg was aching abominably from his first day in the saddle and all he wanted to do was huddle in his thermosac and nurse the hot core of agony within himself in silence.

They were all in a quiet, somber mood, for some reason—perhaps just from the weariness of a long day of hard riding. All but Chastar, that is. The outlaw chieftain was in a heady mood of exaltation; he boasted and swaggered, belching loudly after the meal, cursing the chill edge of the wind—for the air currents here, so high above the surface of the dustlands, could be surprisingly strong—and he became offensive in his manner toward Zerild. The dancing girl endured his lewd gestures and coarse remarks in moody silence as long as she could, then rose and stalked away to make her bed at the far edge of the crater. Usually she could fend for herself in these verbal exchanges, and could puncture Chastar's boastful swaggerings with an adroit and stinging remark, for she knew where all the soft places in his armor were. But tonight she was silent and withdrawn, and, somehow, vulnerable.

Thaklar gazed after her, an unreadable expression on his hawk-like face. Almost a yearning expression, thought M'Cord. He wondered what thoughts were passing through the mind of the other. Then he dismissed it from his mind, rolled over and slept—the deep, numb slumber of the bone-weary.

It must have been just before dawn when the dream came.

104

They were riding—riding. Not down a road but through time itself. Back into the past, the centuries flitting past them like the miles. And as they rode ever on, the world became younger around them. Blue foliage sprouted where there had been naked, sterile rock and sand. A strange green sea lapped to the limits of the horizon, where only the endless dustlands had stretched before.

There were ghosts along the way.

They frowned or grimaced or howled soundlessly. A few laughed; a few watched them ride by with indifferent, uncaring eyes.

But all gestured—*go back.*

Ahead of them . . . was it a wall of mist? A dim, shadowy cloud that rose at the end of the Road of Millions of Years: a cloud, on this cold, empty world where no cloud had ever been glimpsed by man before?

Then the cloud resolved itself into a . . . Face.

Huge and awesome and solemn was that Face. It towered to the zenith of the heavens, and blocked all their way ahead.

It was beautiful, that Face, with a beauty that was beyond that of the flesh. Cold and utterly perfect—like a thing carved by a masterly skill into cold, flawless stone.

Only the eyes lived in all that expanse of perfect beauty.

And the eyes . . . warned!

He awoke drenched with icy sweat, shuddering in the clammy embrace of an unknown and nameless fear. He had awakened just a little before the others, for they were stirring and mumbling. He raised himself up on his elbows and peered ahead, across the level expanse of pitted and riven stone in the direction in which they were traveling . . . the way to Ophar the Holy, if legends were true. There was nothing to be seen in the pale light of a frosty dawn; the surface of the plateau stretched away into the illimitable distance like the top of a stone table built for Titans. It was vacant in the icy dim light.

Why, then, did he still quail in the cold breath of some nameless and inexplicable fear? He could not say. His rough, adventuring life had hardened him to peril; seldom did he feel the clammy touch of fear as he felt it now. Just a bad dream? Perhaps . . . or perhaps it was that keen, fine-honed sense that warns of dangers lurking near but unseen . . . that sense every adventurer, every explorer, must develop within himself if he is to survive.

But now the others were stirring. He yawned a jaw-cracking yawn, climbed out of his sac, and put his night-fears behind him. A bit later, hunched over breakfast, he thought he caught a shadow of fear in the cat-like eyes of Zerild and in the surly gaze of Chastar. Had they shared the same dream, by some odd coincidence or curious magic? M'Cord shrugged and put side such unsettling notions.

None of them knew for certain exactly what lay ahead of them at journey's end. It would be foolish to worry before any cause for worry presented itself. Time enough, when the moment of peril actually came, to be afraid.

All that long day they rode west across the roof of the vast, stony plateau. Jogging wearily in the saddle, nursing his aching leg and resolutely thinking about nothing, M'Cord happened to be riding beside Inga. She was still fresh, staring around with wide eyes, drinking in the experience and tasting its newness. She had exchanged only a few words with him during the whole of the ride, but he could feel her excitement and curiosity, and it amused him in a sour sort of way.

Long years of wandering through the dustlands and across the tablelands of ancient Mars had leached away all novelty in the experience for him. But he could guess how strange and wondrous the journey might seem to one newly come to Mars and to whom its strangeness and alienage had not yet grown stale. Actually, nowhere on Earth was there a geological formation remotely similar to this Sabaeus Sinus Plateau, across which they rode. Once, long ago, this had been a peninsula which thrust deeply out between the equatorial ocean and a long, land-locked bay. Even then, perhaps, it had been level land with few hills, if any, to mar its regularity. When the oceans shrank and dried to salty puddles, what had been a peninsula became a mighty barrier of rock thrusting up some hundreds of feet above the dead sea bottoms. Whatever topsoil had once covered the rocky surface of the peninsula had long since crumbled to dust and been blown away to mingle with the talcum-fine dust of the dead ocean's floor.

On Earth there were plateaux, but however smooth of surface they might once have been, aeons of wind and rain had worn vast crevices and chasms into them, had shaped them into rough masses of crumbling stone. Nothing like this sheer, unbroken expanse of level rock could be found on Earth—if, indeed, anything like this had ever existed on that warmer, greener, more sunward world. But Mars has little or no weather: no seas for the hot sun to evaporate into clouds, bringing rain; no powerful climatic variations to cause winds or storms. What little air there is is thin and cold and dry, and the sun is too dim and cool, from Mars's greater distance, to warm it. Once rock-stratum has been exposed, it remains virtually unchanged for millions of years, for in the desert world there is hardly anything to erode it.

It was an oddly unsettling thought. The rock across which their lopers paced had stood here, virtually un-changed, for perhaps a billion years. Only the craters, large and small, deep and shallow, which pockmarked the stony tableland, were new. For the millions of micrometeorites that peppered Mars annually, as they peppered Earth, were not vaporized by the thin air as they were in Earth's thicker, more oxygen-rich atmosphere.

His loper shied as a pebble was dislodged under its feet. That pebble might have been there for a million years or more before he came riding by to make it move.

And it might remain where it was now for another million years before being dislodged by the foot of a man, or being, yet unborn.

XIII. Under Two Moons

That second day they covered many miles. The long, loose-jointed strides of their ungainly scarlet steeds devoured the leagues tirelessly. In so unvarying a landscape, one had few visual reminders of the distance a day's journey consumed. Had their party been composed of Earthsider explorers, it would have been necessary to employ surveying instruments to ascertain their precise position—devices quite similar to the sextants employed by sea captains back on Earth in the days when ocean vessels were still being used for transoceanic voyages.

But the denizens of Mars, M'Cord knew, have an uncanny sense of distance and location and require no mechanical aids to tell them where they are and how far they have come. Back on Earth, it took sea voyagers thousands of years to perfect a method of discovering the exact location of a ship at sea. Dead reckoning was all very well, but an accurate measurement of precise degrees of longitude had to await the eighteenth century, when a canny Yorkshire carpenter perfected the marine chronometer and solved a problem that had baffled some of the finest intellects of all time, from Ptolemy and Mercator to Huygens and Cassini.

But the People required no such instrumentation to locate themselves upon their world. As if by some sixth sense, they have at all times a precise sense of position and distance traveled. Earth scientists who have studied their ability in this regard account it indeed as something in the nature of a sixth sense; to be precise, they believe that the Martian natives have a sensitivity to declinations in the magnetic field of their planet, which nature has denied to her children on Earth.

They made camp again on the second night after leaving ruined Ygnarh, leg-weary and saddle-chafed and ferociously hungry. It is next to impossible to build a fire on Mars, which is due as much to the absence of wood or brush as to the thinness of the atmosphere, which is so starved of oxygen that it is not easy to keep an open fire burning.

Earthside tourists or colonists solve this problem by using canned foods whose containers are equipped with a heating element: you crack the seal and wait a few minutes, while the food warms itself to the proper temperature. The natives scorn such things as examples of the devil-magic of the accursed *F'yagha*. But even they enjoy a hot meal when they can get it, and colonial entrepreneurs have made a fortune selling cheap, durable heating units to the People. These are simply flat-topped, stubby cylinders of a durable alloy which contains a solid-state energy cell or battery and a dial which can be set to different intensities. You can cook a meal atop one of these units, or boil coffee, or cluster around it as you would around a campfire on the plains of Wyoming. The energy cells are charged with energy in its "static" state and you can "store" as much energy in them as you might wish to—

enough to cook a hundred meals or a hundred million. With no moving parts, except for the vernier dial, there is nothing to wear out, and the units literally last forever. Or for a human lifetime or two, at least.

For all his saddle-weariness, M'Cord found it impossible to fall asleep right off, as was usually his way. The nearer they got to their mysterious destination, the jumpier he got, it seemed.

The others seemed to feel increasingly uneasy, too. Chastar was as nervous and edgy as a cat; and, cat-like, spat and snarled and showed his claws at the slightest provocation. Zerild drew inward and seemed haunted by brooding fears. As for the hunched little renegade priestling, he drew inward as well, hiding his thoughts behind dull opaque eyes and stolidly enduring the curses and occasional blows Chastar dealt him. The two Swedes felt the ominous tension in the atmosphere, too; there were dark circles under their eyes and Nordgren stuttered and stammered and cleared his throat with every word, and he kept tossing and turning all night long.

Only Thaklar seemed unaffected by the eerie dread that came to grip them all. Whatever he felt he hid behind an imperturbable mask of unshaken calm. He kept to himself, exchanging few words with anyone, and seemed to have no trouble sleeping.

M'Cord wondered if the Hawk prince knew better than they what lay before them. . . .

Irritable and edgy, his legs aching from a day in the saddle, the big Earthman finally climbed out of his sac, fastened up the pressure seams on his thermalsuit, and thought to stretch his legs a bit. He moistened his throat from the canteen in his gear and went over to warm his hands before the heat unit. It was then that he noticed another of the party was unable to get to sleep.

It was Inga. The blond girl sat on the edge of the bowl-shaped crater in which they had camped, hugging her

111

knees and staring up wistfully at the stars. The sky was black as India ink, the stars in their countless thousands as huge and brilliant as jewels. Far more stars blaze in the heavens of Mars than were ever seen on Earth, even from the mountaintops or the driest desert. This, he knew, was also caused by the difference in atmospheric density between the two worlds. The Martian air is blurred by no cloudbanks, thickened by no mist of moisture, as are the fair blue skies of the distant Earth.

She either heard him stirring or glimpsed him moving from the corner of her eye, for she turned her head and watched him without speaking; so he climbed the ridge to where she sat crouched and murmured something about not feeling sleepy.

"Neither do I, although I'm so tired," the girl said. She looked up again at the night sky. "So strange," she said faintly, "to see a sky without a moon."

He grunted and sat down near her. "Mars has two of 'em, actually, but you'd never know it for looking. They're up there somewhere, though. The Martians can see them, even if we can't."

"I know," she said dreamily. "What a strange notion . . . invisible moons!"

"Oh, they aren't really invisible," he scoffed with a grin. "Just don't reflect enough sunlight for us to be able to see them. The telescope jockeys have a word for what's wrong with 'em, but I forget—"

"Albedo?"

"Yeah, that's it—I think. Low albedo. The sun's so far away we don't get much of its light as it is, and the moons have such a low albedo that what little light they do get they don't reflect much. Oh, they can be seen, I guess, but you got to know exactly where they are in the sky in order to get a look. And that complicates things even more, because one of 'em, the bigger one, Phobos, moves so fast it goes around the planet three times in a

112

day. The other one, Deimos, hardly seems to move at all; they aren't either one of 'em very big, you know; a dozen or fifteen miles across, at most."

She nodded politely, just as if she hadn't read the whole explanation in the tourist guides.

"Everything is so still here," she said, glancing about. "There's no wind . . . no sound at all, hardly. I wonder why the outlaws don't post a guard at night to keep us from getting away . . . or from . . . trying to overpower them while they sleep."

M'Cord grinned, teeth startlingly white in his dark-tanned face. "Nowhere for us to go to even if we did get away," he said. "And, well, when it comes to tryin' to overpower Chastar and his pals—I guess you never tried to sneak up on a sleeping Martian! Back on Earth, I understand the scientists still haven't made up their minds whether or not the natives here are descended from cat-like ancestors, just as we're supposed to be descended from ape-like ancestors. They sure look enough like cats, with those green-yellow eyes they have, and that silky fur atop their heads where we got hair, and the way they move, graceful and easy, like dancers. But I could tell the scientists a thing or two: there's a cat back there in their evolution somewhere, because they sleep with one eye open, or it seems like that, anyway. Ever try to surprise a sleeping cat? Well, you got about that much chance to sneak up on one of the People! Take Chastar down there: right now he's sound asleep, but if I got within fifteen feet of him, he'd be wide awake—and I'd be starin' down the muzzle of his gun! Nope; no need to post guards; a Martian has a good one half of him on guard *all* the time, awake *or* sleeping! And if you think we ought to have guards posted on account of predators, well, there's nothin' up here on top of the Sinus big enough to bother us. Sandcats and such like, they mostly live down in the dustlands or the gorges that cut deep notches along the

113

edge of a Sinus; you know, caused by cracks in the crust of Mars when she began drying up. Down there in the gorges is where the predators live, because that's where the small critters live that they make their meals off of. Besides, Chastar has a 'buzzer field' set up around the outside of the camp. A subsonic field, to scare away anything that just *might* be out and huntin' . . . we can't feel it 'cause we're inside it. But anything that just might be out there, wandering around and up to no good, will feel it in its bones—and in its teeth, too, just like a king-sized tooth ache. . . ."

His voice died away; suddenly he felt uncomfortable and even self-conscious. It was quite a speech for a man generally as closemouthed as M'Cord was, and he realized it and shut up.

But the girl had sensed it, too, and looked over at him with a queer expression. The softness of the starlight blurred the lines of strain and weariness and tension that marred her beauty by day; suddenly he was very conscious of her warmth and nearness. Her face was a pale oval by starlight, her calm blue eyes curiously tender, and starlight glimmered in her golden hair, striking little witch-lights among the tendrils of that gold.

She smiled at him. "My, you're an odd person, Cn. M'Cord . . . days go by on end and you hardly speak more than three words . . ."

He grunted, and flushed beneath his deep space-ray tan, and was suddenly grateful for the dimness of the unmoon-lit night, which hid his blush from the eyes of the Swedish girl. His volubility surprised even himself. But there is something in a man, even a man of few words, like M'Cord, that enjoys opening up on a subject with which he is familiar when his attentive audience is a slim young girl with tender blue eyes and blond curls spilling about her shoulders.

He suddenly felt as shy and awkward as a schoolboy—

114

and hated himself for feeling that way! He lurched to his feet.

"Umm. Well; guess it's time for some shut-eye, anyway. 'Night!" he mumbled, and limped back to his sleeping place, feeling uncomfortable and embarrassed. The girl looked after him with a small, quiet smile of amusement.

It had been a long time since anything had amused her. All at once she felt young and free and clean and pure again. She enjoyed the feeling, while it lasted.

XIV. The Broken Land

Up until this point in their journey, the way had stretched smooth and unencumbered before them. Due to his innate racial sense of direction and positioning, Chastar had unerringly led them across the smooth tableland of ancient rock. The worn disc of silver which bore the Road marked out like a map was consulted only when they had to work their way around a crater or an occasional deep crevasse.

But with dawn on the third day of the adventure, they rode into rough country. The going became hazardous and difficult and rather complicated; and it got worse the further they went. For here, at some unknown period in the remote past, meteorites had rained down upon the Sinus with unprecedented force and in considerable numbers. The way they followed was riven asunder by crater upon crater, large and small, and the ground underfoot was covered with a loose, treacherous layer of crumbling and powdery rock.

To further complicate the situation, they had by now reached that portion of the Road where Zerild's silver map was blank and smooth and unmarked. From this point forward on the journey, only Thaklar could guide them.

117

And not one of them but wondered, deep in his heart, if the Hawk princeling could be trusted to guide them correctly to their goal and safely around whatever dangerous places there might be, or what hidden man traps the ancient Martians might have set.

M'Cord rode in the forefront of the expedition, a little ahead of Inga. Here the path wound through a narrow passage between the ringwalls of two major craters which were positioned close to one another. So he rode forward all alone.

He was sweating inside the thermalsuit, was M'Cord; and he was very conscious of the pressure of their eyes against his back. The others waited to see whether the ground would open up beneath the pads of his loper and hurl him to a quick death at the bottom of a steep and unseen precipice; or whether he would fall victim to some uncanny enchantment or spell cast ages ago upon this narrow defile that wound between two steep walls of rock.

He was wondering about it, himself.

Just how far *was* Thaklar to be trusted with their lives —with *his* life? Just how fanatical was the Hawk princeling, and to what extremities would he go to protect the hereditary secret of his House, and to shield The Holy from defilement at the hands of renegades and Outworlders?

It had been damned shrewd of the outlaw chieftain to order M'Cord forward alone, the Earthman thought grimly. The lives of the two Scandinavians were of no particular value to Thaklar—he neither liked them nor hated them, but remained stolidly indifferent to their fate. But the life of his brother was another matter. . . .

Or was it?

M'Cord sweated and cursed to himself, and urged the reluctant *slidar* forward. Here the walls of ragged rock nearly closed together, and the passage was so narrow that there was only an inch or so of space on either side. If ever there was a perfect place for an ambush or a trap, thought M'Cord, this was it.

Once through the throat of the passage, the Road widened out a bit and M'Cord relaxed and started breathing once again. He began thinking about just how much Thaklar prized his life as opposed to how much he prized the unbroken secrecy of the sacred Valley of Ophar.

The water-sharing ritual—actually, too simple to be called a ritual—had been performed between an unconscious man dying of fever and one who pitied him and would not stand idly by and watch him die without striving to aid him. Was it then, M'Cord wondered, a true rite of brotherhood that existed between him and the Hawk prince? He wasn't sure; the People, he knew, were great experts in their canon law. They argued the finer points and the knottier questions of law and ritual for the sheer fun of it: to them it was an intellectual game, a mental exercise, like chess or mathematics or Bach fugues to Earthmen. And he had no doubt that ample precedents could be quoted by Thaklar to invalidate the rite between himself and M'Cord.

Then again, just how important was it to Thaklar to preserve the secret of the Valley Beyond Time? Surely he put the value of the secret above his own life. Would he not put it above M'Cord's, even though he accounted the Earthman his brother?

M'Cord shrugged, consigned all such nagging questions to hell, and put the matter out of his mind.

There was no point in trying to figure out what Thaklar thought.

And he had enough to worry about, as things were.

The country was rising now; they were winding up an unmarked trail that led to the crest of a slope. This steep rise must have been the ringwall thrown up by a gigantic meteor ages before. Hurtling out of the depths of space a billion years ago or more the meteor had struck in the exact mathematical center of the Sinus. The atmosphere had been many times richer in oxygen then, and the heat of the meteor, hurtling down through the envelope of air at thirty-five thousand miles per hour, had ignited the air. The surface of the peninsula had turned to molten slag; the impact crater could well be many miles across. M'Cord knew enough about elementary physics to know that a meteorite only ten feet in diameter can strike the planetary surface with the force and fury of the hell bombs that vaporized both Nagasaki and Hiroshima long before his grandfather had been born.

The meteor that made the Ophar crater might have been no bigger than that.

They had traversed the length of the Sabaeus Sinus by now, and had reached the exact center of the Meridiani, a great, squarish mesa that grew like a knob at the end of the peninsula. They were just a couple of degrees south of the Martian equator now, and exactly on the prime meridian.

What they might find here, no one knew; no one could even predict. Only the Timeless Ones, as the Martians termed their ancient gods, could say.

Climbing the slope of the outer wall of the crater grew increasingly more difficult as it grew ever steeper. They had been forced to leave the pack-beasts below, but remained in the saddle, since *slidars* trained for riding can climb as well as a man and are as sure-footed as any mountain goat. And it would have been grueling and perhaps impossible for them to have attempted to scale to the summit afoot. Especially for M'Cord; not that Chastar cared about M'Cord, of course.

The pack-beasts had been unburdened and turned loose to wander where they wished. Chastar grumbled at the necessity, but there was really nothing else to be done.

The footing became dreadfully insecure. For here, on the sides of the vast cone of the crater, meteorites of smaller size had peppered the crater walls with pockmarks. Craterlet was superimposed upon craterlet, and, beneath the cosmic bombardment, the naked rock had been reduced to gravel, which the ages had pulverized still more. The powdery stone grit, intermixed with pebbles, made the worst conceivable footing for the lopers.

Eventually, finding themselves sliding back three yards for every yard they gained, they dismounted on Chastar's order and went forward one by one on foot, leading the *slidars* by their reins. They inched their way up by walking sideways, gaining a better purchase in this manner, since the human foot is longer than it is wide.

Thaklar guided them with minute care. Many times he bid them pause while he pondered his memory for landmarks. Leg-weary and tight with tension of unseen dangers he sensed but could not see, M'Cord wondered how any landmark could survive a couple of million years unaltered. Evidently they had, for although Thaklar had to stop and cudgel his memory and search with his eyes, he nonetheless guided them forward without error or turning back to trace another path. Either the landmarks had not eroded out of all recognition in all these aeons on a weatherless planet, or maybe it was the work of the gods that had somehow preserved them intact. M'Cord neither knew nor cared. He wished it were over, and that he could rest his leg.

The crater wall continued to rise beneath them. They were far above the surface of the Sinus now, and could look back for scores of miles in the clear, dry air. The crater must have been as high as Fujiyama, M'Cord thought wearily; and he wondered as to its breadth. He wondered if it were not wider even than the monster the Earth scientists had marveled at in the days before Christoffsen

121

had made the first landing—the incredible supercrater the NASA scientists had named Nix Olympica.

On a broad shelf of rock they rested and broke the midday fast. They were bone-weary and gasping for breath, even Chastar and Zerild. The atmosphere of Mars is thin enough on the dead sea bottoms; on the mountainous heights it is virtually nonexistent.

Zerild was examining the worn disc of ancient silver.

"We are almost beyond that place the inscription calls 'the Broken Land,' " she decided. Chastar grunted around a jawful of dried lizard meat.

"Broken indeed is this land," he grumbled. "Half a hundred times I thought my boots would slip and that I would lose my footing and roll all the way back down again. A man could die here from a slip of his foot."

He squinted up at Thaklar, who sat a little apart from the rest of them, munching his meat and staring up the slope. The eyes of the Hawk prince were wide and thoughtful, but his features were inscrutable.

"*Hai*, Hawk! I misjudged you—I, Chastar, admit it! *Jehu*, but I dreamed you would betray us all to our deaths in the Broken Land, once you were become our only guide. Why did you not, eh? Speak! Would you join with us in the treasure? Is that it?"

Thaklar eyed him with cold eyes, aloof and disdainful, his expression somber.

"There was no need for me to betray you," he said at last, "for you will betray yourselves in the end, aye, all of you."

Chastar puzzled over this enigmatic prophecy and decided that he didn't like the sound of it. Snarling an oath, he hitched his gunbelt around so that he could toy with the handle of his black leather whip.

"Who will betray Chastar?" he demanded. "Not the woman, for she is mine, or will be, and no woman betrays Chastar and lives! As for the aged one, he knows very well the name of his master, and has felt the weight of his hand ere this, eh, snake?" he said with a harsh, ugly laugh. He loved to bait the little renegade priest, who was deathly afraid of him.

Phuun veiled his eyes and bowed his head obsequiously. Chastar laughed again, this time boastfully.

"What mean you then by such foolish words?" he demanded.

Thaklar matched him glare for glare, his face impassive, his temper unruffled.

"That is for the future to tell," he said calmly. "But remember this, red wolf! It was written of old of Ophar the Holy, that therein shall be given to each according to his deserving."

The simple words were spoken in a calm, uninflected voice. M'Cord wondered, then, why they seemed pregnant with a terrible and overpowering sense of doom and menace.

III

THE SEARCH
FOR
THE SECRET

XV. Into the Valley of Mystery

The brief rest break was soon over. Chastar was eager to
reach the top of the crater wall before nightfall. They were
all very tired, for it had been a long day and already they
had come about seventeen miles. But Chastar would hear
no word of rest or delay.

So they began again. It was not as hard going as before,
for here the slope was naked rock alone, with neither
rock dust nor loose pebbles to make the footing insecure
and dangerous. But it was an almost constant upward
climb, and the way grew steeper and steeper with every
yard.

In the brilliant dry clarity of the thin air, from his
height, you could see the entirety of the Meridiani Mesa
and a dim, blurred glimpse of the dustlands that ringed it
on three sides. This must be one of the highest eleva-
tions on the planet, thought M'Cord. He was sweating
again: whatever the mystery of Ophar was, they were
about to get their first glimpse of it.

Thaklar led them by an almost invisible trail, from
outcropping to outcropping. He warned them to place their
hands and feet with great care in precisely the positions he

showed them, for the stony shelves were loose in places and one mistake could be fatal. It was a long way down.

There was no point in trying to lead the *slidars* up so steep a slope, and they no longer had need of them. Chastar fumed and cursed, but there was nothing else to do but unload the beasts and turn them loose to find their own way down to the base of the crater wall, to join the pack-beasts. From below, the rising ground level had been so gradual as to be imperceptible, and had he known that the terrain would change in so abrupt and perilous a manner, he would have abandoned all of the beasts below with supplies of food, to await their return. But he had not known, and Thaklar had not seen fit to apprise him; so the lopers were set loose to slide and clatter back down the slope to where their brethren wandered.

This meant that unless the beasts somehow lingered in the vicinity, they would have to walk back to Ygnarh when the time came to return. There was no help for it, but it enraged Chastar to the point of fury. The Hawk prince made not the slightest response to the storm of curses and imprecations that broke around his head; he merely waited until at last Chastar was silent, his temper spent, and they could continue on the last leg of their journey.

The climb continued. Now the slope was extremely steep indeed; the way led up an almost vertical wall of naked stone.

They took it easy, with frequent pauses to catch their breaths. It was even more difficult than it had seemed from below, the final ascent. It took them more than three hours to make it to the top.

Here they found a broad open space, as wide as a highway, but littered with enormous boulders as big as aircars. The rock-strata here ran in crazy fluid lines, like solidified molasses. This rock had been molten lava a billion years before; and the impress of the tremendous

128

forces that had shaped it were still clearly visible on this desert world where there was nothing to erode the stone and erase or soften the curvatures into which the molten rock had cooled and hardened.

They made their way through the litter of boulders. The top of the wall was as smooth and flat as the crest of ancient battlements in some Cyclopean fortress built by prehistoric giants.

Chastar and Zerild were in the lead. They inched sideways between two huge boulders that stood close together, with only a narrow space between them. Beyond the narrow space they stopped suddenly, as if frozen with shock.

Zerild drew back with a startled gesture.

Chastar sucked in his breath sharply; it hissed between his clenched teeth.

They were standing on the very edge of a precipice. Only two inches beyond their feet the wall fell away in a sheer cliff that dropped hundreds of feet to the floor of the shallow valley below.

The others joined them; they stood, side by side, on the brink of the abyss and looked down on Ophar.

"What devil's trickery is this?" Chastar rasped hoarsely. But no one answered him.

M'Cord, his bad leg hurting him abominably, was the last to join them at the brink of the valley. He looked down . . . and found it hard to believe the testimony of his eyes.

Below them, the floor of the valley lay at a distance of five or six hundred feet straight down. It was shallower by far than he had expected.

And it was nothing at all like what he had expected.

The valley floor was partly drowned in inky purple shadows by this hour of the afternoon. And the floor itself was difficult to see clearly; but it stretched away to the other side of the crater wall, a distance of about twenty

129

miles, he estimated. So it was only half as big as Nix Olympica, after all.

Roughly in the center of the crater, about ten miles from where they stood, a conical center peak rose from the crater floor. It was the impact crater left by a giant meteorite, then, as he had guessed. Only impact craters have that pyramidal-shaped central peak.

These things he only noticed in passing, as it were. It was the floor of the valley that held his attention, as it held that of Zerild and Phuun and Chastar and his brother. For it was nothing more than a broad and level rock-field littered with crumbled boulders and pocked with innumerable small craterlets.

It was dead, dry, sterile, lifeless rock—just like the surface of the plateau they had been crossing all these days!

It was nothing like what he had imagined it would be.

That made him stop and think. Exactly how had he pictured Ophar? Well, as a valley paradise, he supposed: a beautiful garden. But that was nonsense; there were no gardens on Mars, for the planet was old and dead and barren.

Why, then, had he pictured it so? Probably because of the parallel between Ophar and Eden; a garden is a garden, after all.

But he should have known better.

So should they all. For it was patently obvious that the others had shared much the same dream as M'Cord. Zerild stared down at the dead, rock-strewn valley with an expression of great surprise and disillusionment. Chastar was in a rage, his mouth working loosely, his body trembling with violent fury. Even Phuun was shocked from his customary torpor: the renegade priest was slack-jawed with a surprise so enormous as to be more properly termed horror.

"Tricked! I've been *tricked!*" yelped the outlaw. He

130

turned on Zerild and struck her a vicious blow with his open hand, catching her off guard. The blow left vivid red splotches across her cheeks.

"You devil's slut! You and your babble of maps and lost marvels! You did this to me—*you!*"

Thaklar cleared his throat. Chastar turned; the Hawk prince was pointing at the inner surface of the cliff. They looked—all of them, even Zerild, nursing her stinging face with murder burning in the depths of her green eyes.

A stairway had been cut into the stone cliff, leading down.

"That is the way down, Chastar," Thaklar said calmly. Of them all, only the Hawk prince seemed undisturbed by the disillusionment of finding the Valley Where Life Was Born to be a lifeless and empty place of barren, dead rock.

"Down! Why should I wish to go down?" snarled the outlaw. "There is dead rock and dust aplenty back the way we came; should I, then, descend into the crater for more of it?"

"If the Valley is truly a dead place, then why this stair?" Zerild asked wonderingly.

It struck them, then, the oddness of it.

With enormous industry and effort—*someone*—had cut the rocky surface of the sheer precipice into a zigzagging flight of stone steps. Stone steps that led down to—nothing?

It was not possible. Nor was it believable.

As if not trusting their eyesight, they turned simultaneously to peer down into the shallow valley once again. But it still looked the same, a sandy rock plain strewn with worn and crumbling boulders, irregularly pockmarked with craterlets of varying size. There was not the slightest trace of vegetation to be seen among the litter of stony fragments, or upon the slopes of the further wall.

131

No glint of moisture, no sign of ruins, no evidence that man had ever walked that shard-strewn plain. Only a dreary and desolate valley filled with emptiness.

Then why had the stair been cut in the wall?

Chastar spat a curse, but his fury left him. In its place was a hard, cold-eyed determination.

"Shoulder your gear, all of you," he commanded. "We are going down!"

"Into . . . that?" Nordgren questioned feebly, the level afternoon light glinting off his eyeglasses. "But there is nothing there!"

"There must be something there, or they would not have cut the steps into the wall so men could reach it," Chastar said grimly. "I have come too far and endured too much to turn back without seeing for myself exactly what Ophar truly is. Only when I have paced that plain from wall to wall and found nothing, only then will I give up the search and turn back. Shoulder your gear, *F'yagh,* and begin to climb down. You will lead us, yellow-hair; you and your kinswoman!"

Nervously, Nordgren peered down at the first step of the stair. It was only a few inches below the brink on which he stood. The stone of the cliff surface had been cut away, and each step projected about two feet from the side of the precipice. It was narrow enough, the stair, but by going slowly and watching your step it should be safe enough to descend. Shrugging, the Swede helped his sister down, cautioned her to be careful and not to look down into the abyss lest she become dizzy.

Then he stepped down onto the top step, tested it for security, found it strong enough to bear the burden of his weight, and strode down after his sister.

One by one, they followed him.

It was not as difficult as it might have been. There were no winds to shake them; no mosses or lichens underfoot to make their bootheels slip; and none of them was bothered by vertigo or a neurotic fear of heights. And the stair was beautifully smooth and straight-cut, with a shallow, easy decline where it could have been steep.

So they began to make their way down into the Valley . . .

The Valley Where Time Stood Still.

The Valley Where Life Was Born.

And they wondered why this empty and desolate place had ever been thought holy, and why it had been forbidden to men for all these ages. . . .

XVI. The Descent

One by one, in single file, they climbed down the ancient stone stair that led to the floor of the crater.

The steps were cut into the side of the rock cliff in such a manner that they slanted to the south for a distance of about twenty-five yards, then terminated in a squarish stone platform where one might pause and rest a bit, catch one's breath, before continuing the descent. From the first platform, the stone stair angled back in the opposite direction for another twenty-five yards, and again there was a platform where they could again pause before resuming the descent.

M'Cord's leg was aching abominably, but he gritted his teeth and clamped his jaws shut and refused to whimper. Favoring his bum leg as best he could, he limped, in the rear, more slowly than his companions. There was nothing else to do; Chastar was in a frenzy of impatience to see the crater floor for himself, and would brook no delays.

At the first landing, M'Cord rested and sipped a mouthful of water, taking the opportunity to down a few painkillers. Thereafter he managed to drag himself along from step to step, although rather slowly. But they were all weary and none of them felt like sprinting down the stairway.

Nordgren was marveling over the ingenuity of the stonework.

"A magnificent achievement!" he panted, watery blue eyes peering about through his spectacles. He cleared his throat nervously. "What amazing engineers the ancient Martians must have been—think of the sheer cumulative man-hours of labor spent in hewing such a stair from the solid rock! It's an extraordinary feat; yet one cannot help wondering for what purpose it was designed. Obviously, there is nothing within the crater that a man would wish to see. . . ."

Thaklar grunted impassively, but a hint of humor glinted in his hawklike eyes. "You trust too much to sight alone, *dok-i-tar*," he commented. "There are things that cannot easily be seen, even by one whose eyes are strengthened by bits of glass."

Nordgren blinked owlishly.

"Eh? Well, perhaps so; we shall see. But I cannot help wondering just how these steps were hewn. You will observe there are no marks of chiseling left in the stone: the surface and sides of the steps are smooth and regular as sanded wood. This can, of course, be accomplished even by primitive stonecutters, but only with enormous effort. It puzzles me that they should bother to smooth and polish the stone in such a manner."

"Perhaps the stair was not hewn with chisels, but by another means," Thaklar suggested.

Nordgren looked at him with bafflement. Then his thin lips quirked with amusement. "Well, actually one *does* get the impression the stone had been reduced to a fluid condition and cast, somehow, into the desired configuration! But such skill would, of course, have been beyond the powers of a primitive people."

Thaklar made no reply. But it was Phuun who answered him; the little renegade priestling seldom spoke, and hardly ever exchanged a word with any of the three Hated Ones. Nevertheless, in this instance he spoke to Nordgren.

"The People were never primitives," he whispered hoarsely, the glint of fanaticism in his snakish eyes. "The Timeless Ones, who raised them to manhood from among the squalid brutes, nurtured in their breasts the arts of a high civilization. Who is to say what powers were not possessed by our ancestors, who, in this very place, walked with eternal gods?"

Nordgren blinked and made a feeble protest, which Phuun ignored. There was no credible answer the scientist could make to the arguments of religious belief, so he wisely kept silent.

M'Cord had a hunch that they would find other marvels down here somewhere—marvels that would reduce the incredible craftsmanship and engineering of the stone stair to the level of child's play. But he held his tongue and concentrated on the labor of keeping on his feet and moving down, one step at a time.

Inga paused to catch her breath, pressing back one errant blond curl with the back of her hand.

"I should have thought we would be at the bottom of the stair by now," she said faintly. "It only looked to be five or six hundred feet down."

"It's a good thousand or more, if it's a foot," her brother said. "The cliff goes down and down—see?—the foot of the stair still looks as far away as it did from the crest of the crater wall!"

"But how can that be?" the girl asked bewilderedly.

Her brother seemed agitated. His eyes gleamed with mounting excitement as he glanced about intently.

"I don't know! I don't understand any of this. There's some queer distortion of lightwaves here . . . some queer

137

optical effect I don't understand. Look at the valley floor—it looks *different* than it did from above!"

They followed his pointing hand, all of them. Indeed, a peculiar change had come over the bottom of the crater. By now they had climbed down the zigzagging stair some hundreds of feet. And from this perspective, the floor of the crater looked oddly . . . *wrong*.

M'Cord squinted down, trying to puzzle out what it was about the vista of barren sand and broken stone that had changed as they had descended. Then, with an uncanny thrill of premonition, he grasped what it was about the bottom of the crater that looked different now.

It was curiously blurred and artificial-looking. It was rather like a skillful painting by one of the extinct impressionist school; seen at a fair distance, the objects depicted by the painter are visible with great clarity of realistic detail. But when you come close to the canvas, the objects within it dissolve into mere meaningless blurs and splotches of raw color. It is the perspective of distance that resolves them into realistic detail.

It was rather like that with the Valley. The sweeping vista below looked oddly . . . *unconvincing*. Like a painted stage backdrop. The change in perspective, as they came closer to the floor of the Valley, exposed the flaws in what now appeared to be some manner of optical illusion.

They stared at one another in tense silence, a dawning wonder in their eyes.

Then they started down again, with Thaklar and the outlaw chieftain in the lead.

As they came to the bottom of the stair, or what appeared to be the bottom, at any rate, the optical illusion became blatantly obvious. There was no longer any question but that the stony floor of the crater was a false vision of some kind—a trick of light, designed to fool the eyes at a distance. Here, from the bottom landing, a dozen yards above the crater floor, the illusion was exposed as a hazy blur which twisted and distorted the lightwaves. It was like the level and motionless surface of a lake; but a lake of stationary *mist*.

"Hell!" M'Cord gasped. "It's a mirage!"

Thaklar did not answer. He was testing the illusory floor of mist with one booted foot while Chastar lingered a bit above him, staring down with wide, incredulous eyes.

The moment Thaklar's extended leg encountered the blurry surface of the illusion, *it went completely opaque*.

Then it became perfectly reflective, like an enormous mirror. The travelers stared down at their own inverted images, and at the crazily upside-down reflection of the stairs and the cliff. It looked as if they were dangling over the edge of a monstrous abyss at whose bottom there was only dim purple-black sky, with the first stars glittering beneath them.

The effect was horribly unsettling. Inga stifled a gasp of dread and clutched her brother's arm for support. Zerild moaned deep in her throat and covered her eyes. Vertigo seized them all—it seemed that to move an inch off the stair would be to fall down into the weirdly inverted sky.

Thaklar withdrew his foot with an air of having answered a question he had been asking himself. And as he did so the illusion changed again, assuming its former aspect—that of the dim, blurred, strangely distorted image of a stony crater floor, barren and lifeless and littered with bits of crumbling stone. Only this time they knew that the image was not real.

"The magic of the Timeless Ones," Phuun whispered in awed tones.

"Nonsense!" Nordgren snapped nervously. "Some curious effect of nature is at work here. Perhaps the meteorite is still imbedded in the floor of the crater—an aerolith of some unknown mineral whose mass is tremendous, causing a distortion of light. Or perhaps the meteor is radioactive, affecting our eyesight, interfering with the normal transmission of visual images . . . but, surely, it is nothing supernatural!"

Thaklar turned his gaze upon the outlaw chieftain, who stood as if transfixed with amazement and, perhaps, fear.

"This is the moment of decision, red wolf," the princeling said in quiet, measured tones. "You can turn back now and live. Go back to ruined Ygnarh in safety and resume your former manner of life, and all will be well. But to descend further is to go forward into the unknown. The Timeless Ones have placed all of the Valley under interdiction: this barrier of illusion which they left behind to mask the reality of Ophar forever from the knowledge of men tells us that the power of the Timeless Ones, to bless or to curse, to cure or to kill, still lives in this holy place, and is still strong. Turn back, Chastar, and forget your mad dreams—they are blasphemy! No one will call you coward if you turn back now."

It was the wrong word to apply to Chastar.

He stiffened, glaring. One hand flew to the butt of his energy gun; with the other he gestured curtly to Thaklar to stand aside.

"Chastar fears neither man nor beast—god nor devil! Stand back—I have not come this far only to turn my back on the greatest treasure in the world!"

And with those words he stepped past the place where Thaklar stood, descended to the very bottom of the stair— and sank into the quivering veil of illusion—

And disappeared.

XVII. Beyond the Barrier

There was nothing else to do but follow him. One by one they filed down the narrow stone stair and passed the place where Thaklar stood silent and grim, his eyes somehow pitying—and entered the veil of quivering, mirrorlike mist. And one by one they vanished utterly from sight.

M'Cord paused to Thaklar, who smiled briefly at him.

"Yes, go on, my brother! I think you and I have little to fear from what hides below. The powers that still guard this Valley will know that we were forced to come here against our will, and seek nothing of the treasure that the outlaws hope to find. You and I, my brother, may live ...*unchanged*."

M'Cord puzzled over the use of this cryptic word, but there was no time now to linger and ask questions. He was possessed with the same overmastering curiosity as to what lay below the barrier of illusion that had driven the others to dare its mystery.

He descended, step by step. When he touched the shaking mist-mirror a peculiar thrill ran along his nerves. It was like a faint electrical charge—numbing, a slight, chilling shock. Nothing painful, but more than a bit startling.

The mist came up and drowned him. For a moment he felt himself completely blind; but the smooth stone steps were still there beneath his feet. He felt his way down, step by step, descending into complete darkness.

Out of the darkness, light blossomed.

A dim, dreamy haze of light, soft and faintly golden.

As he descended beneath the barrier, a vision of strange marvels appeared. It was like a bit of stage legerdemain, or one of the miraculous transitions the old-time moviemakers knew how to work. The scene was transformed, instantly and completely, as by some mighty magician.

He stood on a steep slope of rock overgrown with a carpet of soft moss. Sapphire-blue was that moss, and it deepened to metallic indigo and brightened to lucent azure as the shifting light played across it.

A warm, humid gust of air met him, dampening his face and filling his lungs with the perfume of strange, unearthly flowers.

His bootheels slipped in the sapphire moss which carpeted the bottom steps of the stair. He slipped—slid—lost his balance and fell. The thick, rubbery cushion of moss broke his fall, but he slid down the inclined slope until at last he dizzily came to a halt amidst strange flowering bushes of azure foliage that bore long frond-like leaves resembling those of terrene ferns.

He lay there panting for a time while his lungs adjusted to the warm, moist air.

He looked up. Above him, about forty feet over his head, was the sky. But it was not the dull, purplish-black sky of desert Mars, studded with hard, diamond-bright stars. It was a hazy sky of limpid jade-green, shot through with glints and gleams of lucent gold. There were no stars in this strange, new sky, and no sun, either. And the ringwalls that surrounded the crater had also vanished.

He looked down, and for the first time saw the Valley as it really was. He stood at the lip of a vast cup of glimmering blue. Thick woods of gnarled and knotted trees grew near the sides of the cup, thinning out toward its center, some miles from his position, They were unlike any trees he had ever seen or heard described before, their boles built up of tangled, serpentine black lengths, like twisted roots grown thickly together into a column. The black wood glistened wetly with an oily sheen, and the foliage borne up by the writhing branches was like glimmering ribbons, with silver undersides and metallic blue outer surfaces. They wavered in gusts of humid breeze, the ribbony leaves, like the drooping fronds of an Earthly willow tree.

Between the knotted boles dense blue grass grew thickly, starred with tiny, white, seven-petaled flowers, and be-spangled with dew. The grasses rustled and a curious, small creature came into view. It was lithe and supple, like a cat, but was nearly the size of a cheetah. It was clothed in short fur, colored coppery-red, with immense, fragile, pricked-up ears and oval eyes enormous and jewel-like in its point-chinned, elfin face. The eyes were glowing amber, misty brown depths swimming with flecks of gold.

The cat-creature regarded him calmly, without the slightest sign of timidity. Then it turned from him indif-ferently, stretched with a languid, supple play of muscles, and began to devour a ripe golden fruit that had fallen from the ribbon-leafed tree. M'Cord rubbed his eyes, blinked, and looked about him like a man in a dream. There are no trees on Mars, although deposits of fossilized wood have been unearthed, suggesting the existence of pre-historic woodlands ages ago; and while the canal areas are carpeted with bluish moss, it is thick and rubbery-leafed, bearing little resemblance to this fragile, tender, delicate azure growth.

And the cat-creature was yet another mystery! Why

did it not fear him, a stranger, potential danger? Finishing the succulent fruit, the beast cleaned its whiskers and delicate paws with dainty licks of a narrow pink tongue, then rose and lazily glided away into the depths of the woods without so much as a backward glance.

"Amazing . . . simply amazing."

He turned. It was Nordgren who had uttered the phrase. The scientist stood some little distance away, half hidden behind dense shrubbery, staring after the cat-creature with a bemused expression on his face.

Noticing M'Cord, he included him in the range of his attention in a vague way.

"You know, some authorities hypothesize a cat-like mammal somewhere back at the beginnings of the evolutionary history of the Martians," he said, half to himself and half to M'Cord. "The creature has been extinct for a billion years, if ever it truly existed at all; a few fossil bones have been found, and a skull or two, but their evidence is fragmentary and inconclusive . . . but, if we can believe the testimony of our senses, here we have a living survival of the remotest ancestor of the Martians, lingering here in this strange and wonderful place. . . ."

"Where are the others?" M'Cord grunted.

The blond man gestured vaguely. "Here and there . . . the outlaw captain has gone into the center of the Valley to investigate the cleared area, which seems to display the signs of deliberate cultivation. . . ."

He wandered off, stooping to examine the leaves and flowers of the bushes. M'Cord heard a sound behind him and turned to see Thaklar on the slope, arms folded upon his breast, staring with brooding, hooded eyes across the Valley.

"It is truly Ophar the Holy, even as the legends describe it," he said in a soft, wondering voice. "Truly is it the lost *huatan* told of in The Book . . . and here, indeed, shall we not find the *Jhay yam-i-Jaah* itself, the Pool of

144

Eternity, where shimmers the Water of Life?" Catching M'Cord's eye, he broke off his wondering monologue. "You look upon the sacred place of the People, Outworlder whom I call my brother. Here it was, a billion years ago, the gods walked among men . . . among the First-born, whom they raised to manhood out of the red murk of bestiality. . . ."

His voice broke off and he gestured suddenly for silence. A strange, ululating call rang vibrantly through the green-gold dimness, dying in shuddering echoes. It did not sound like the cry of a beast, nor even of a bird, if birds existed in this strange Edenic land. There was a hissing to it, a sibilance, that was curiously alien and menacing.

A peculiar expression stole into the yellow eyes of Thaklar.

"Is it possible? But, after all, why not? . . . if the Valley is here beyond the Barrier, and the beasts and flowers . . . then why should not the Guardians truly exist, as well? Come, 'Gort my brother, we must go down into the gardens! Quickly, lest these rash, presumptuous fools intrude upon a mighty mystery and bring doom upon us all!"

Unquestioning, M'Cord joined him. They strode into the strange woods. Dense, blue-green gloom closed about them; dewy grasses rustled underfoot. Gusts of exquisite perfume assailed their nostrils from strange flowers, pallid and luminous as lillies, with immense gossamer petals as frail and delicate as lace. Jeweled eyes peered at them from shadowy boughs; but there was no fear in those eyes, and no alarm, either. They merely observed, tranquil and uncaring.

Thaklar and M'Cord entered a woodland glade. Here a small stream ran, meandering through the grove. Inga knelt on its grassy banks, looking at the reflection of her face in the flowing waters. The eyes she lifted to them were dreamy and vague; gradually they cleared and she smiled hesitantly.

"Who could ever have guessed this grim, cold world had such a place in it?" she murmured.

Almost as if in answer to her query, there came a liquid, birdlike trill from the depths of the shadowy woods. Thaklar gestured fiercely for silence. The Swedish girl got up and came to stand by them; they stared into the depths of the gloom as if sight alone could penetrate to its uttermost recesses and read its mysteries.

A girl and a boy stepped out of the woods to face them. They were children, perhaps thirteen or fourteen at most. Their slim, ambiguous pale-gold bodies were nude of clothing, or adornment, except that the girl wore huge red flowers, like hibiscus, woven into her long dark hair. The boy was naked but in one slim hand he held a spray of blossoms.

The children stared at them wonderingly, chattering to each other. Then the girl pointed at their garments, which were dusty and travel-stained, and she burst into a liquid trill of laughter, wherein the boy joined his pure tenor to her clear, bell-like soprano.

They stared back at the naked children, so innocent and unashamed, as if unaware of any reason to cover themselves. They were slim and graceful and diminutive, the boy with the sleek, short furcap of a Martian male, the girl with a long cataract of silken black hair that fell to her small, rounded bottom. Their faces were laughing and elfin, with huge eyes, slightly slanted, amber-golden.

Thaklar addressed them in the Tongue, spoken universally across the face of Mars. The children listened, tilting their heads at the sound of speech, but made no answer.

"Why . . . they twitter and chirp like—like birds," Inga said slowly. "It's like they had never heard of language, and only use their voices to sing and chatter with. . . ."

The girl's eyes widened as the green-gold light glim-

146

mered in Inga's blond hair. Her soft, full, rosy lips pouted into a wondering expression and she uttered a single-toned, bell-like note. Then she glided forward and extended one slim, golden arm to touch the older girl's bright hair with a delicate caress. Inga sought to speak to the child, but she paid utterly no attention to her words, absorbed in the shining locks of blond curls.

The boy's attention wandered. He curled up on the grass by the edge of the stream, plunged long, slim arms up to his breast in the gurgling water, and began to pick the huge, blue, lotus-like water flowers, whose stems he wove into a circle about his narrow waist so that the wet flowers drooped across his slender thighs. He giggled and shivered at the cold wetness of the flowers, then rose lithely and began dancing idly about the glade, the flowery wreath swinging about his naked loins.

"They look like teen-agers," M'Cord muttered in a low voice, "but they have the minds of little children. . . ."

Now the girl's attention wandered from Inga's hair. Like a slim gold sprite from some ancient fresco, she glided to the edge of the wood and vanished therein without a backward glance, as indifferent and uncurious as had been the cat-creature M'Cord had seen earlier.

The naked boy, suddenly bored with his loincloth of water flowers, ripped them away from his middle and let them fall to the blue sward. A moment later his slim nude form glimmered from sight as he wandered off into the depths of the forest in a different direction from that which the girl-child had taken.

M'Cord shivered. Such childishness and innocence were unnatural and vaguely sinister. Those eyes of luminous amber had been bright but soulless: it was as if there was little mind behind them. They were—*vacant*.

He felt suddenly cold. If this was Eden, why should he all at once feel—afraid?

XVIII. *The Gardens of the Ushongti*

An hour or so later they came out of the woods and into
the central plains of Ophar.

The woods shaded by imperceptible degrees into the
mossy meadows. Slowly, as they came through them,
glades became more frequently interspersed with clumps
of the curious serpentine trees with the blue-and-silver
ribbony leaves. Then small clumps of trees broke apart
the stretches of mossy glade. Finally, only lonely groves of
six or seven trees stood here and there to mar the smooth,
meadowlike appearance of the verdant plain.

They had wandered some six or seven miles into the
center of Ophar by this time, M'Cord guessed vaguely.
Where the rest of their party had strayed, he had no idea.

Ahead of them, across the meadow in the distance
toward the center of the Valley, stood a ring of trees. For
lack of anything else to make their goal, they set out for
the trees.

M'Cord's leg still felt numb and dead, but it no longer
ached. Indeed, he felt fresh and vigorous in a way he had
not experienced for a long time. The air of the Valley
was richer in oxygen and denser in moisture than the air

anywhere else on the planet; that alone, perhaps, could account for his delicious feeling of well-being.

The depth of the Valley was beyond guessing; a thousand feet below the rim of the crater, perhaps two thousand, perhaps half a mile or more. There was no way of telling, but they had been traveling downhill, or down a very gentle inclined slope, for a very long while. It was obvious that the denser, richer air at this depth was the result of the vegetation. On Mars, it seemed, as back on Earth, vegetation exuded pure oxygen: the effect was like that in a pine forest, where the air seems purer and fresher than elsewhere. It seems that way because it *is* that way; there is perceptibly more pure oxygen in a pine forest than elsewhere. And, if the illusion-barrier was a natural thing, caused by something like an inversion-effect, doubtless that would tend to trap the moist, heavier air within the depths of the Valley.

He looked up at the strange and fascinating "sky," which was the illusion-barrier when seen from beneath. Imagine a sky like a pool of lucent and pallid green, shot through with weird ripples of luminous gold that tremble continuously in motion; that is the uncanny sky of the Valley.

They approached the ring of trees. They were six or seven deep, and were situated with odd regularity, evenly-spaced, almost as if deliberately planted in that manner. They were curiously different from the trees the adventurers had passed in the forest. For one thing, the knotted and serpentine tangles that made up their trunks were glossy red, rather than glistening black. And for another, they—*moved*.

The graceful, willow-like branches stirred continuously with a subtle, snaky motion. This caught M'Cord's attention from the first, once he had limped near enough to see them clearly through dim twilight haze. But what sent a chill of alarm through him was the fact that although the

150

curving, slender branches undulated with a constant, slow, stirring—*there was no wind here to cause that movement!*

And as soon as they had stepped within the circle of trees, M'Cord became aware of unseen eyes upon them. His companions felt the invisible scrutiny of hidden watchers, too; Thaklar growled and shivered, his furcap rising in hackles, yellow eyes darting intently from side to side. The girl Inga shivered too, and drew closer to the two men, her eyes, enormous in the weary pallor of her face, shadowed with a dim fear to which they could none of them put a name.

It was not so much that the unseen eyes were threatening. They caught the impression of a benign but wary attention; that which observed them did so narrowly, uncertain as to whether they were friend or foe. Was it the trees themselves?

If so, M'Cord felt better once they had passed through the ring of trees and had penetrated into the middle.

And here stood . . . *a garden!*

There was no other word to describe it. Flowers grew, pale and delicate and huge, in carefully tended beds; streamlets, clearly artificial, meandered between the blossoming shrubs and poured tinkling over miniature waterfalls. M'Cord noticed that there were no withered flowers, no dead stalks, no fallen petals to mar the silken smoothness of the sapphire moss that grew here thick and soft. It was as if the hands of the invisible gardeners carefully plucked up or unrooted all imperfections, all signs of decay.

"The Gardens of the Ushongti," Thaklar murmured, half to himself, in wondering tones. "But—where are the Guardians?"

Ushongti.

M'Cord knew what they were: the guardian genii of the old myths. He had seen their fabled likeness carved on marble gates and stone monoliths in the dead cities many

151

times before. He recalled their features. Like brooding giants they were, with savage tusks hooked over lipless, gashlike mouths, and immense glaring eyes; he recalled to memory their traditional three-horned brows, which always reminded him of Neptune's trident, and their elongated ear-lobes. Surely, Thaklar did not expect to meet shadowy giants out of fairy-tales—?

But then, why not? After all, this very garden was something from the ancient myths. And if it was here, then why not the weird ogres as well?

They came upon a still lake or pond, filled with placid cool water—the source which fed the wandering rivulets. And there beside the margin of the pool they came upon an artifact—a statue carved from glittering scarlet stone in the likeness of a huge, fat-bellied lizard, dozing in the sun.

Then it turned its head and looked at them. . . .

Some time later—hours, perhaps, but it was difficult to tell in this dim twilight vale where there were no dawns or dusks, no noons or nightfalls—Nordgren came wandering in. He looked dazed and flushed and feverish; so distracted was he that he barely noticed that his sister was with Thaklar and M'Cord.

He sank down, trembling with excitement or exhaustion, on the soft carpet of blue moss beside them and accepted with absent hands the huge ripe fruits Inga passed to him from the bowl out of which they had lazily been eating. He was talking to himself in some language M'Cord did not recognize—perhaps his native Swedish. He seemed so distracted that he scarcely reacted when the Old One came waddling up to offer them more of the pale, thin, honey-hearted wine they had been drinking.

The huge, depthless purple eyes observed him tranquilly, then turned to M'Cord.

. . . The others will be here soon, three of them, two males and one female . . . we are calling them in, as we did this one with the bright hair. . . .

"I know; thanks," said M'Cord, nodding.

The thin, cool voice that had whispered these words into his mind without need for oral speech ceased. The wise, humorous purple eyes observed Nordgren gently. *. . . He seems in a daze, perhaps his mind is injured, or has he a sickness? . . .*

Inga answered, in a mild, amused voice, that her brother was often this way. The Old One shrugged philosophically—a gesture startlingly human, M'Cord thought—and began to pour the wine, squatting back on its haunches like a curious idol of red stone—like the statue they had thought it to be at first glimpse.

Odd, thought M'Cord, watching the grave lizard-creature with lazy affection, how close the Martians had come to catching the likeness of the Ushongti in their carvings. The great, solemn, humorous eyes they had transformed into glaring orbs of menace, of course, and they had exaggerated the golden, trilobed crest into fierce horns, but the arms, with their curious, four-fingered paws, they had remembered properly, and the great swelling paunch that made the scarlet lizards look so comical that it was impossible to fear them. Once the conventions were fixed in the canons of art, M'Cord guessed, they tended to be reproduced over and over without change or adaptation for countless ages. And it had been a billion years since any of the Martians had seen an Ushongti, the Old One had gravely informed them.

Nordgren sipped absently at the wine in the stone cup Inga had handed him; gradually his bewildered, unfocused gaze cleared and he began to come out of the dazed stupor. He blinked at them in surprise.

"Citizen? You here . . . Inga? I wondered what had become of all of you . . . odd that we all just wandered

153

off, the moment we reached the true Valley beneath the illusion—like we were all drunk, or drugged, or something. . . ."

"Yeah. I noticed it, too," said M'Cord with a lazy yawn.

"A trauma—that's it—a traumatic shock, the sudden transition to this strange, bewildering place; and the extraordinary amount of oxygen in the air, must have made us exhilarated, heady . . . bemused . . ."

He broke off to gape at the Old One, who sat on its haunches, arms folded comfortably across its fat paunch, its short, stubby tail thrust out behind it so that it sat like a kangaroo. After a while Nordgren remembered to close his mouth. He was unstartled by the appearance of the huge, intelligent, lizard-creature, and unafraid of it. Natural telepaths, the scarlet reptiles radiate some of their own placid and unruffled calm, and their warm, gentle benignity, to all receptive minds. After the initial moment of awe and wonder, you accept them for what they are— the ageless and undying Guardians of Ophar, left here by the gods to tend the garden and to watch over all that dwell within the Valley.

Inga was sleeping, pillowed on the flowery moss, her face oddly relaxed, sweet and calm and innocent as the face of the girl-child they had encountered wandering naked in the woods. In slumber the harsh lines of strain and worry were smoothed away from her face.

M'Cord yawned, feeling sleepy himself. He had half unseamed his suit, since it was warm and gentle here. No need to unpack the thermo and put it up; better to just lie back where slumber claimed him, and sleep where he lay.

Nothing could harm him, or anyone, in this idyllic place, the Old One had told them. So long as they kept the Peace unbroken.

. . . Your leg has been hurt, terribly, and has mended

154

ill, the calm whisper of the Old One said, deep within his mind; *I will tend it for you, as you sleep. . . .*

"Yeah, you do that; a little shut-eye, now," the Earthman mumbled. Then he stretched out and slept, and in his dreams pale-golden children wandered naked and unashamed through a timeless garden where pain and death and terror could never come.

XIX. Unsolved Mysteries

M'Cord never knew just how long he slept—probably
for ten hours or more. But when at last he woke it was to
find that during the "night" Chastar and Phuun had come
wandering in: "Called in," as the Old One so oddly
phrased it.

The outlaw chieftain seemed strangely sober and chas-
tened, and Phuun himself was curiously different—more
voluble somehow, and less locked up inside himself.
M'Cord had already discovered (without understanding
how or why) that there was something in the very air of
the timeless Valley that changed people in strange and
curious ways. Whether this was due to the humid air,
warmer and richer in oxygen, or to some telepathic effect
broadcast by the Ushongti—or both—he did not even
bother trying to riddle.

Far more surprising than these was the change in his
leg.

During the night it had—healed! Completely. The lead-
en numbness was gone, and the throbbing ache. No
longer did he go limping about, dragging the half-useless
limb behind him like a dead weight. The torn and atro-

phied muscles were limber and supple; the leg had mysteriously and miraculously returned to normal.

Even the scar was gone, the long, ragged, horrible scar left in his flesh where the venomous claws of the sandcat had laid him open from hip to knee. It was gone as if it had never really been, and the flesh was whole, the skin unmarked by so much as a scratch.

Well, the Old One had promised to "mend it" while M'Cord slept; obviously, it had kept that promise!

His leg restored to perfect condition, M'Cord felt euphoric—rejuvenated. He had always driven his body hard, using it, demanding much of it. He had forced it to become the superb, trained, powerful and flexible tool his hard, wandering life required it to be. When the sandcat had crippled him he had felt, twistedly, as if he had betrayed himself somehow. It had aged and soured him; made him bitter; made him feel old and useless. Now all that was changed; and the Valley had worked its first miracle.

But probably not its last, he thought.

Other things had happened during the night while he slept—although "night" was a misnomer in this timeless place where they had ventured outside of time as they knew it, into an enchanted realm where they no longer experienced the familiar gradations of light and dark they had lived with all their lives. Here there were no mornings, noons, or nightfalls . . . only a perpetual and changeless dreamlike haze. A jade-and-topaz twilight, never darkening; a garden frozen, as it were, in eternal amber.

One thing that had happened was The Tent.

Nordgren retained much of the puritanical conventionality of his Swedish bourgeois ancestry. To just stretch out on the sapphire moss and slumber among the flowers smacked of lotus-eating to him; proper, civilized men slept in beds, or at least cots—cots, moreover, hidden within the stuffy privacy of tents. So, wakening a little from the dreamy languor of Ophar, he insisted on un-packing a tent from his gear. He and Inga had erected it while the Ushongti squatted, kangaroo-like, scarlet paws folded together over fat paunches, watching with solemn, puzzled purple eyes the incomprehensible behavior of these Outworlders.

The tent would have looked blatantly out-of-place even in the dustlands or the rocky crevices of the Sinus. Here it was like a coarse subway graffito scrawled across a pediment of the Parthenon.

The tent was an expensive Earthsider tourist setup from Abercrombie-Fitch-Bonwits, all vacuumized nine-ply nio-flex with pressure-seam flaps and electric heating elements sewn in the inner linings. It was as ugly as a homberg on the Apollo Belvedere, and about as useless as a rain repeller in Death Valley. But the proprieties of urban civilization remained uppermost in Nordgren's prim and proper world-view—even in Paradise! So therein he and his sister had spent the night, while the others merely dozed on the azure sward wherever sleep had claimed them.

M'Cord shrugged, caring little. He began to take off his clothes. The pond was real water, cool and fresh and pure—the rarest luxury conceivable on this desert world; and it had been half a year or more since he had enjoyed anything remotely resembling a genuine, no-foolin', honest-to-God *bath*.

To avoid shocking the acute sensibilities of the Swedish scientist, or his sister's, for that matter, M'Cord bathed as soon as he woke. No one, as yet, was stirring, save for a couple of the fat scarlet Ushongti waddling here and there among the flowers, busy on small, horticultural tasks. Under his torn and travel-stained thermalsuit M'Cord wore a long-sleeved, high-necked blouse of plastic fabric —one of the self-cleaning kind that repel dirt and moisture electrostatically when you plug them in a power cell over-

159

night. That and leggings of the same material, and heavy socks, were all an old Mars hand ever wore under his thermals.

Once soothed and refreshed and tingling from a long, lazy dip and soak in the pool, letting the perfumed air blow against his skin and dry it, he felt a peculiar reluctance to get dressed again. In this summery place, where mosquitos had never evolved and even the roses had no thorns, there was no real need for clothing except for reasons of sexual modesty. Stretched out on the soft, springy moss, he stared at his rumpled and disreputable clothes, which he had stripped off in a heap. The golden, carefree children of the wood had the right idea, he thought; and they seemed as sexually innocent as babies, despite their apparent adolescence.

So, when Nordgren finally emerged from within the pointless nioflex monstrosity in which he had chosen to spend a stifling and airless night, it was to find M'Cord stripped to the buff, except for a pair of extra leggings he had trimmed down into scanty trunks. He had discarded even his boots. The scientist was scandalized, but the idea caught on with the others as soon as they awoke and saw M'Cord in his new get-up.

Chastar cut down his woolen *yiog'a* in a skimpy sort of loincloth; but he retained his gunbelt and bandoliers and the ever-present whip that seemed to be a symbol of his masculinity to him. Zerild laughed at M'Cord's near-nakedness and lazily stripped to the nude for her morning plunge, careless of the men who looked on with frank enjoyment. M'Cord watched her, grinning, beginning to understand how she could goad a man like Thaklar into blind infatuation. She was slim and sinewy as a boy, all tawny gold, all silken seductiveness, without an ounce of fat on her: like a slim, lazy, beautiful pantheress, he thought—and just about as deadly.

After her swim—and he wondered where a Martian

160

dancing girl had ever learned to enjoy that Earthsider sport on this desert world—she exchanged her own travel-stained clothing for a skimpy loincloth and all the jewelry she had. The effect was one of barbaric and tempting nakedness; M'Cord liked looking at her, and she seemed to like being looked at. But Chastar, once his boisterous and bawdy jests died on his lips, sat watching her with sweat on his brow and an ugly, devouring look in his hot, narrowed eyes. There would be trouble with Chastar before long, M'Cord thought wearily.

If so, it had been long deferred.

Breakfast was a simple affair of ripe, delicious fruits, a light and delicate and effervescent wine, like sparkling burgundy or dry champagne, and cakes of a dainty, doughy pastry unfamiliar to all of them. The friendly lizard-folk served them on platters of beautifully carved and polished wood; the effect was almost that of a small Hawaiian picnic.

Careful to keep his eyes well away from Zerild, who lay with her long, supple legs stretched out, wriggling her small, bare toes languidly while nibbling on a luscious fruit, Nordgren professed a scientific curiosity in Ophar.

"It's simply incredible, but yesterday I recognized thirteen extinct species, all thriving here although they died out everywhere else on Mars before we were out of the Pleistocene," he said, watery blue eyes glinting with the scholar's fervor behind thick lenses. "Those trees, for example; the flowers—we don't even have *fossils* of them! But most amazing of all are the Ushongti . . . imagine it, Citizen: two sentient races living here in symbiotic relationship; one distinctly humanoid, the other a hitherto unrecorded species of warm-blooded reptile! No one ever dreamed of anything like this. We have known that the ecology of Mars was dominated by reptiles, with the sur-

161

viving mammalian species relatively minor; hitherto it was assumed that this was, simply, that the Martian biosphere began to decline sharply in viability during the Martian equivalent of our own Age of Reptiles—that is, few mammals had even begun to evolve by the time the planet started to die, its seas to dry up, its vegetation to wither, its atmosphere to leak into space as the comparatively weak gravitational field was unable to contain it. But—a race of sentient reptiles: *Telepathic* reptiles! Astonishing."

He burbled on in his stammering, excited way, really talking more to himself than to M'Cord, who paid scant attention, merely uttering a polite, interrogative grunt from time to time. But this last bit caught M'Cord's interest.

"If that's so, Doc, how do you explain the Martians themselves? Seems to me a race of humans, whether evolved from cats or not, takes a long time to work itself up the evolutionary ladder."

Nordgren nodded enthusiastically, lank blond strands of hair flopping untidily over his pale forehead.

"Yes; you have laid your finger on the weak link in the arguments of scientific orthodoxy," he stuttered eagerly. "To evolve to humanity requires a long history of mammalian ancestry—or it ought to, at any rate. But the origin of the Martians is a mystery we have yet to solve, and we have few clues to go on. Some authorities suggest a dramatic mutation—a direct leap of a million years of ordinary evolution between two generations, say. There's something to be said for this, since the thin atmosphere of Mars lets through a lot more hard radiation than does Earth's, thus vastly increasing the mathematical probabilities of mutation. . . ."

He broke off, his gaze wandering into the illimitable distance of the haze-lit Valley.

"Wouldn't it be odd," he whispered, "if the answer

we're looking for turned out to be identical with the secret we came here to find! The natives themselves say their gods molded the First-born out of the stuff-of-beasts . . . that's a literal translation of *jarad-i-zhā* . . . we can dismiss the business about their gods as pure anthropomorphic myth-making . . . the same, familiar, homocentric world-view that gave rise to Prometheus and Odin and Jehovah and other simplistic demiurge conceptions by primitives. But . . . somewhere in this Valley, which seems to lie outside of the reach of time to alter and change . . . we may find the cradle of evolution itself . . . the secret of life."

For no apparent reason, M'Cord suddenly shivered.

It was warm and summery here. Why, then, did he feel the cold breath of the Unknown upon his nakedness?

XX. *The Crystal Grail*

Later on that afternoon, M'Cord got restless and decided to take a walk.

Thaklar had vanished on some ramble of his own; Zerild was napping golden and naked among the flowers, careless as a nymph. Nordgren was off exploring somewhere and, as for Phuun, the little priestling had found the earthenware crocks in which the Ushongti store their fermenting wine, and had drunk himself into insensibility. Nobody knew where Chastar had gone off to. That left M'Cord and Inga.

"How about it? Take a walk?" he invited. "Now that I got my new leg, or my old leg back, or whatever, I feel like giving it some exercise. Want to come along?"

Bent over her brother's notes, which she was transcribing, she looked at him without even really seeing him.

"A walk? . . . Karl says we should stay close to camp," she murmured.

"Let Karl stay as close to camp as he wants to," he grunted. "There's nothing that can harm us here. C'mon; it's too nice a day to waste it scribbling all that stuff."

She regarded him wistfully. "It *would* be nice, but Karl says—"

He made a rude noise.

"That for Karl! All you ever say is 'Karl says . . .' C'mon; you're a big girl now. Let the march of science get along without you for an hour. Let's stretch our legs!"

"Well . . . just for a little while," she said. "Which way shall we go?"

He pointed off to his right, beyond the miniature lake.

"We haven't gone that way, any of us; we came from over there. So let's see what there is to be seen."

She nodded submissively and they started off. M'Cord felt as gay and lively as a boy; not only was it heaven to be free of the nagging pain and the half-dead, crippled leg, but he felt exhilarated in mind and spirit in a way he had not felt in too many years. Normally taciturn, he found himself joking and clowning, trying to coax a smile out of her, to bring a little gaiety into her mood. He wanted to see her laugh. The image of that naked golden girl-child in the wood haunted him; she had been fresh and free, laughing and alive. Inga should be like that, he thought, and wondered what it was in her mind or personality, or in her past, that kept her silent and withdrawn and solemn so much of the time.

She began to sweat in her thermalsuit, which she wore, still primly seamed to the neck-band.

"Why don't you skin out of those hot things?" he asked. She flashed a startled look at him; her expression was so filled with instinctive horror that he burst out laughing.

"Hey, I don't mean you should slink around in your skimpies as bare as Zerild," he tried to reassure her. "But surely you've got something a little cooler to wear?"

"Karl says—" she began, timidly.

" 'Karl says; Karl says,' " he mimicked her tone with a grimace. "Don't you ever say 'Inga wants'—whatever it

166

is that Inga *does* want? You talk about your brother like he was brother, father, and husband, rolled up in one."

Quite suddenly, she was weeping.

Not a sound escaped her tight-pressed lips. But great tears came welling one by one from those limpid eyes, to river down her cheeks. The expression of agony on her face was so acute and so terrible that M'Cord was frightened. Then he softened.

"Hey," he said awkwardly. "I'm sorry. Really, I am! I guess I got a big mouth; anyway, don't pay no attention to me. I didn't mean to make you cry—"

He stopped short, for she had halted suddenly, and he almost blundered into her. She was staring at something out of his line of vision, and her expression was so filled with amazement that there was no room there for agony or tears.

He turned to see what had surprised her . . . *and saw it.*

Some twenty feet beyond where they had paused, a pavilion stood amid the azure moss. There was a circular dais of three steps, which rose from the level of the moss and then declined into a depthless hollow like a vast cup.

It was roofed with a smooth, rounded dome, that cup; and the dome was held high by seven slender pilasters, spiral-fluted like the horns of unicorns.

Carved entirely from pure, dew-clear crystal was that pavilion—three-stepped dais, cup-like bowl, spiraling pilasters, and hollow dome. The dome was cut and polished like a gigantic lens; the crystal of the dome bent awry the dim fall of light in a torrent of illumination.

Beneath the lens of the dome, the cup was like a grail cut from pure crystal.

It was filled to the brim with—*glory!*

Imagine pure white light, intolerably brilliant. Imagine that immaculate radiance somehow—*curdled*—into a liquid. Imagine that incandescent white liquid whipped into a froth, a seething foam of beaten light.

That was what they saw in the crystal grail: a grail filled to the brim with foaming light!

They stared—rapt—exalted!

A feeling of standing in a holy place stole upon them; they had almost knelt before the crystal grail, but something restrained them.

It was filled with glory, that place. A freshness was in the air, like the air of April gardens washed clean by an April rain. Joy rose up within them, for no reason; their blood sang in their veins. Their minds were filled with joy, and the fragrance of the rose of Eden was in their nostrils.

They felt young, exuberant—light—free. They forgot about their bodies, did not feel the heaviness of their meat, the sordid gurgling of body fluids, the muffled pump and squeeze of the heart, the lungs bloating and deflating like absurd, fatty bellows. They felt like pure spirit—exalted, flushed with joy, filled to the brim with light as the crystal pool was filled.

They knew what it was, of course.

Jhay yam-i-Jaah; the Pool of Eternity, wherein seethes forever the glorious Water of Life. . . .

A thousand legends proclaimed this place was holy. A thousand ages sanctified it as once on another world was sanctified another Garden, and a Tree.

The eternal gods of Mars had walked here once, a billion years ago.

Here had they made man, the Timeless Ones. Molded him into being out of the flesh of beasts. Instilled within his brain the divine spark of reason and intelligence that blazed up through the red murk of bestiality like a star shining through the roiling smokes of war.

They were holding hands, like children, without knowing it.

They turned to look into each other's eyes and saw there the same wonder and awe that was in their own.

Then, in that marvelous daze that had come upon them,

168

they clung to one another, seeking comfort in the animal warmth of body against body in the unbearable presence of supernal Mystery.

They kissed, and clung.

And then her brother was there, his face white and wet and working, his eyes wild with rage and horror, damning them weakly, in a stammering voice that poured fourth filth like stinking ordure in the white radiance of that holy place where they had found the Water of Life. And found each other . . .

The Old One told them something about it, but not much. It was not that the lizard-creature refused to answer their questions; it was that they did not know the right questions to ask.

Bubbles—or something very like bubbles—broke constantly from the foaming glory to drift idly on the breeze like globes of trembling and insubstantial light.

. . . *Avoid them lest they touch your flesh,* the calm whisper echoed in their minds. *For they do work strange transformations upon men, making them young again.*

"Is that bad?" murmured Chastar, half to himself, with an eager, leering grin.

"The golden children we met in the outer precincts of the Valley!" Nordgren stammered. "Have they been touched by these—these bubbles?"

. . . *Many times,* the Old One whispered gravely. *Some of the childlike ones have been here from the Beginning, returned to youthfulness again and again by drinking of the Water . . . others came here as you came, seeking the Source of Life and the Mysteries thereof. They were incautious and drank too deep, and became as children again, even in their minds . . . for the Water robs the mind of its memories, even as it robs the body of its years . . . therefore, hearken unto me, and beware!*

169

More than this the lizard-creature would not tell them; in fact, it seemed reluctant to discuss the Pool at all. And now that the matter had been brought out in the open, they began to notice the bubbles it had warned them against. Now and again they were to be seen, floating about idly, drifting on the breezes. They wandered about the dreaming garden, quivering globes of opal luminance, frail as a vapor, exquisite as a moth. The six avoided them and were careful not to be touched by one of them, fearful of the results.

Nordgren was on fire with excitement. The discovery of the Pool was of such transcendent importance that it took precedence even over his fury at having discovered M'Cord and his sister in an embrace. The living fossils alone had excited his scientific curiosity to a high pitch—the Valley, he said, was somehow immune to the hidden forces of change and development and age and evolution. But the mysterious fluid of the Pool solved that riddle, while posing another of even greater magnitude.

"Doubtless the liquid is highly radioactive; perhaps it contains some hitherto unknown isotope in suspension . . . something that works directly on the glands, slowing or even reversing the cumulative process of glandular breakdown we call aging. But, if it works on men and beasts, might it not have the same effect on vegetation? Trees and flowering plants have nothing resembling the glandular secretory systems found in the higher mammals, but they do have a built-in aging system . . . the bubbles that drift from the Pool must touch them in passing, rendering them young and ageless, too. Think of it!" he whispered, his pale, ascetic features rapt with fervor. "These trees and flowers and bushes, which represent unknown or long-extinct species, may be each of them millions of years old!"

170

XXI. The Theft of Eden

Late that same afternoon, prowling about restlessly, M'Cord found the little priestling, drunk as usual. He was propped up against a boulder grown thick with azure moss, starred with small, brilliant flowers like minute gems. The Martian blinked sleepily at M'Cord, who paused by him.

"Hi, Phuun. You missed it. We found the Pool," M'Cord grunted. Something gleamed, quick and sly and furtive, in the slitted, opaque eyes of the other, and was gone.

His wrinkled features broke into something which was probably supposed to be a smile. He giggled, offered M'Cord a ceramic bottle of the champagne-like wine. Nothing loathe, the Earthman accepted it and stretched out on the mossy turf.

"Soon now, it will be very soon . . . we knew we would find it, you see," the old priest mumbled. He was very drunk—so drunk that he probably didn't know it was M'Cord he was speaking to.

"What'll be 'very soon now'?" M'Cord inquired, taking a long swig from the earthenware bottle.

Something glittered and was gone again in the little man's vulpine eyes.

"Our power," he whispered. "We shall be kings, the red wolf and I. Aye, and greater than kings! No holy Jamad has ever wielded such power as we shall have. There will be lives to play with, the destiny of nations to fondle like toys. We shall be as gods, the wolf and I . . . gods!"

M'Cord eyed him quizzically. On the chance that the wizened little priestling was actually as out-of-his-mind drunk as he seemed to be, he tried a question on him.

"Phuun, you're a priest, or you once were, anyway. Why have you, of all people, been hunting Ophar? There isn't any treasure here—we haven't seen any gold or jewels or anything, yet, and I'll bet there aren't any to be found. So what did you hope to get here, anyway?"

The renegade priest giggled again, and wiped his mouth with the back of one bony hand.

"Power . . . and youth," he muttered, as if to himself. "The greatest treasure of all . . . power, such as no man has ever dreamed of since the world was young. And immortality . . ."

"Immortality?" M'Cord repeated the word skeptically. "Is that really so important?" He thought it was pretty damn important, himself, but he hoped to draw the little tosspot out and get him to talking freely.

Phuun took a long pull from his bottle and when he took it from his lips and lay back gasping for breath, his eyes were vague and haunted with some memory, some taint of an emotion which M'Cord could not clearly read.

"To be young again . . . never to die . . . *aiyii!* Gods, never to cross over the Bridge of Fire and stand before the Three who slumber forever in Yhoom! . . . Never to stand, naked and alone, before the Timeless Ones, for . . . *judgment.*"

There was something in his voice when he hoarsely whispered that last word that made M'Cord's blood run

172

cold. If it was fear, it was a fear so enormous, so utterly hopeless, that it became a terror.

He blinked hazily up at M'Cord, as if finally seeing whom he had been speaking to.

"Aye, *F'yagh*. . . I have done those things in my toll of days that makes me dread the Place of Judgment . . . for I, who was once a Servant of the Gods and privy to Their Laws, know all too well the . . . *the price that I must pay for that which I have committed!*"

His bright, fearful eyes went vague and dim again and slid away. He mumbled brokenly to himself, his wrinkled face a mask of dread and sorrow, clinging with trembling hands to the bottle as a drowning man might cling to a bit of wood.

He shivered, as if suddenly cold.

"I fear, *F'yagh*. I fear to grow old, for then death is near, and after death I must go down to judgment before They Who Slumber in Yhoom . . . and too well do I know the price and the punishment They will exact from me for that which I have done. But, to grow young again, and ever-young! To stave off death, forever! Never to see the hour when my poor spirit is riven from its house of flesh, and scourged across the Bridge of Fire to stand naked and helpless before the Timeless Ones! . . . For that, *F'yagh*, I would dare any blasphemy; for that, *F'yagh*, I dared come even here to The Holy, to Ophar, against the interdiction of the gods!"

His voice died to a mumble again, and M'Cord had to bend close to his thin lips to hear his words.

"You have never sinned as I have sinned, *F'yagh*! Never done that from which your own soul shrinks, shuddering, in loathing . . . so that, in the end, you come to hate yourself . . . for that you have become the epitome of all that you ever despised or condemned in others. . . ."

His voice died away, he lay there muttering brokenly to himself, oblivious to M'Cord's presence. The Earthman eyed him askance. He could almost find it within him to feel sorry for the old man, even to pity him a little.

M'Cord's had been a hard life, and the code he lived by was a hard code. There was little room for pity within him; but it seemed natural to him, lying there, watching the twisted face of the wretched thing which had once been a priest, to pity that which it had become.

Something the old man had mumbled earlier nagged at him. He rose on one elbow and caught the drunken man's attention.

"Phuun—why will just finding the Valley and the Pool give you and Chastar so much power? This place is forbidden to men—shunned by them. To have reached it at all is a sin against your creed, so how do you expect to wring power from something like that?"

The rheumy eyes of the old man wandered about and suddenly focused on his face. The withered face broke into a smile so cunning, so gloating, that it could only be described as ghastly.

"He who holds the secret of The Holy," the renegade whispered hoarsely, "holds power naked in his hands. Think, fool! This vale—this garden, and all that it contains—is sacrosanct to the People! From the white pole of the north to the white pole of the south, there is no man nor woman who would not lay down life itself to protect the preciousness of Ophar from . . . *desecration.*"

The word hung there between them. It seemed to echo in M'Cord's mind, repeating itself endlessly, over and over.

Phuun smiled. The smile was sick with self-loathing, but there was an ugly, twisted sort of triumph in it, too.

"The word shall go out from here to the Nine Nations that the wolf and I and his woman hold mastery over The Holy. If the faithful among the People do not wish us to defile the sacred places with blasphemies so irrevocable as to forever desecrate Ophar, they will yield power over

174

themselves into our grasp, and we shall command them . . . and they shall obey us in all things . . . for we hold to ransom the Valley Where Life Was Born. . . ." He began to laugh.

M'Cord stared at the tittering little thing with unbelieving eyes.

This was what the outlaw and the renegade priestling had meant by "treasure"!

To have captured the *huatan* of Ophar—to hold it under threat of defilement until the Nine Nations capitulated to their demands! The enormity they contemplated was beyond belief: it was a blasphemy so immense as to almost defy description.

M'Cord got to his feet shakily and went away from where Phuun lay, sodden with wine, gloating over a sin that sickened even himself.

He had no religion, had M'Cord; not even the Neo-Christian creed in which he had been born. He gave no reverence to any gods or to any church. But this was a private thing, a matter that lay between himself and his own soul. And he felt no contempt or derision for the faiths of other men. Indeed, he felt a certain degree of respect for the ancient worship of the Martians, whose religion was older than all the creeds of his own world by millions of years.

Even to him, the sin of Chastar and Phuun was an unholy thing. Even he shrank back from what they contemplated with disgust and horror. It was as if a sect of Moslems had plotted the theft of the Black Stone from Mecca—the holiest relic from the holiest sanctuary of all Islam!

It was as if renegade Christians somehow schemed to hold for ransom the Garden of Eden itself. . . .

Suddenly he knew he had to find Thaklar, to tell him the enormity of Chastar's plot. For if the soul-sick priest and the half-mad outlaw should succeed in their fantastic coup, they would seize control over the very planet itself. They could plunge the desert world into a holy war so devastating as to be beyond belief. They could strike a death blow to the heart of an ancient civilization.

They could destroy a world. Or drive it mad!

IV

THE PATH
TO
PEACE

XXII. Shadow over Eden

He headed back to the central gardens, to the area about the pond where the six generally made their base. He went recklessly, leaping over small streams, blundering through the flowerbeds, careless of being seen.

Thaklar could have no inkling of the incredible thing they planned, the outlaw and the fallen priest. The gloomy, grim predictions of the Hawk prince might or might not be proved true—the gods, whose invisible presence yet seemed to linger over this holy place, might strike down the desecrators by some miracle. Or they might not. . . .

Therein shall be given to each according to his deserving . . .

It was a conforting thought, that strange phrase Thaklar had quoted from The Book back on the slopes, once they had come through the Broken Land unscathed. It seemed to imply that the Valley could take care of itself—that Ophar was not without its own defenses.

Well, maybe so, M'Cord thought. But there was a coldness in his guts, an uneasiness in the back of his mind. Eden itself had needed an angel with a flaming sword to

179

guard its gates from those who would enter therein. And they had seen no angel here. . . .

What had Thaklar said back on the rim of the crater? M'Cord recalled the scene to memory with difficulty; so much had changed since they had come through the Barrier of Illusion, so much was different in this enchanted, timeless garden, that memories of what had gone before were vague and dim, like memories of a forgotten life.

Chastar had said he must have misjudged the Hawk, that he had thought the princeling would have betrayed them on the Road. And Thaklar—what had he said in reply?

There was no need for me to betray you, for you will betray yourselves in the end . . . all of you.

Well, maybe the unseen forces that watch over the Valley will mete out punishment and reward, M'Cord thought. And maybe not. Heaven helps those who help themselves: it was an old saying back on Earth, M'Cord knew; and he suspected that there was still something to it even here. Fatalism is all very well—for fanatics. But M'Cord had always made his own way, never expecting anyone else would do it for him. And that hard rule applied even here in the Valley, surely!

The ungainly tent Nordgren had put up loomed in front of him. Never had it seemed so intrusive, so out of place, as here and now. A sudden cold, inexplicable thrill of uneasiness went through M'Cord.

Maybe the Valley could defend itself against intruders.

But, if so—could it discriminate between the evil and innocent?

To eradicate the hideous threat to its tranquility that Phuun and Chastar represented—might it not destroy them all?

If the unseen guardians struck against the desecrators—

180

would they stay their hand against those who planned no desecration?

M'Cord had a horrible suspicion that they would not. The angel with the flaming sword does not weigh motives in the balance of judgment. She lifts her blazing brand against those who would enter Eden from innocent scholarly curiosity, and those who would gain entry from the blackest and most despicable of motives.

Against Thaklar. And M'Cord. And Nordgren.

Against—*Inga!*

He hesitated, unable to decide what to do, who to warn first. He was confused, not knowing what was going to happen, but grimly certain that *something* was. Maybe Ophar could defend itself and maybe not—but could they risk the chance? So many myths about this place had now been proved true. Maybe that ominous phrase from The Book was also prophetic.

The only thing to do was to get out now, before the slumbering guardians of the Valley . . . woke!

What was that cry?

Startled, he lifted his head, questing from side to side as a beast does, scenting danger on the wind.

A woman's voice—muffled, but audible.

A woman in pain . . .

He turned toward the Nordgrens' tent. The garden seemed to dim, as if there stood a shadow over Eden; as if something that had long slumbered was now—awake!

He unseamed the tent-flap and looked within.

And found himself in a small, tight, private hell.

She had taken off her thermalsuit and stood there naked to the waist. Her back was to him and she was bent over, clinging to the mainpole with both hands. They were not tied, those hands, he saw with a sick feeling deep in his guts.

181

Her back and shoulders were bare and white and smooth. Her firm breasts hung loose as she bent before the switch.

The switch in the hands of her brother.

His back was toward M'Cord, but every time he drew back for another blow, M'Cord got a glimpse of his face. It was the face he had seen before, when Nordgren had discovered them embracing by the Pool.

It was slick with sweat, that face. The mouth was open, the lips drawn back from the teeth in a ghastly grimace that was more like the snarl of a beast than a human smile.

The eyes were hot and feral. A beast's eyes are more sane. These burned with a sick joy, a twisted ecstasy.

The switch with which he flogged her had been torn from one of the bushes. It laid red lines across the tender whiteness of her back and shoulders. With every slow, stinging stroke the man gasped a hoarse phrase, repeated over and over, jerked from the core of his being:

"... *kissed* him! ... *touched* him! ... *embraced* him! ... *fondled* him! ... like a bitch in heat ... animal! *Animal! Kissed* him! ..."

The girl was not bound to the mainpole, but she did not try to avoid the lashing blows or to get away. Her body shuddered, wincing involuntarily at every stroke. From time to time a muffled whimper, a faint, choked cry, was wrung from her tightly closed lips. But she did not try to evade the whipping.

He could not see her face, could M'Cord. It hung down, hidden beneath the damp tousle of her blond hair. He was glad, at least, not to see her face. For perhaps her eyes, too, held that sick ecstasy that burned in the eyes of her brother.

M'Cord stood watching for one frozen moment of shock.

Then he stepped forward, snatched the wet switch from Nordgren's hand, broke it and flung it away, and drove his balled fist into the center of the fearful, astonished, furious face Nordgren turned upon him. Teeth snapped with a soul-satisfying crunch under his blow. The other man stumbled back and fell with a bleating cry.

Face grim-set, M'Cord strode to where Nordgren had fallen, got a handful of his garments, dragged him to his feet, and hit him again.

"No! Don't *hurt* him!"

Inga flew between them, her eyes filled with terror, and stooped over her brother, who lay moaning through bloody lips.

M'Cord watched without expression as she raised his blond head upon her white breast and touched his bruised mouth with tender, trembling fingers, crooning wordlessly to him.

He made a growling sound of disgust deep in his throat and turned to go.

Inga sprang to her feet as if to say something, perhaps to plead that he keep their guilty secret to himself. Behind her, Nordgren staggered up to sit on one of the cots, his face ravaged and haggard with some emotion to which M'Cord did not try to give a name.

Maybe Thaklar was right; they would destroy themselves.

They had found no Serpent in this Eden. So they had brought their own evil with them.

He half turned to say something to the girl . . . he could never recall what.

But then it happened.

Through the open tent-flap drifted a shimmering bubble of trembling opal light.

It was frail, that floating, insubstantial sphere. A dimly luminous globule which blurred with changeful, rainbow hues. It drifted past M'Cord; it drifted to Inga, who stood immobile, arms outstretched—

It drifted into the valley between her breasts and vanished!

The change that came over her, the swift, magical transition, was incredible.

As her flesh absorbed the floating orb of glimmering light, the lines of care and worry, of pain and tension, faded from her face. Fright and shock and alarm died in the depths of her blue eyes. They were, for the first time since M'Cord had known her, calm and sweet and innocent.

The dark stains of guilt and shame were gone from them: they were as pure and clear and happy as had been the amber eyes of the naked golden children of the woods.

The dark emotions and terrors erased from her weary face made her seem ten years younger. The white oval of her features, framed in tendriled gold, glowed with an inner serenity—with a free and joyous purity such as M'Cord had seldom seen in a human visage. Sometimes you saw that glowing, happy calm in the carved features of a Buddha, but seldom in the face of man or woman.

She looked down at herself wonderingly. She still wore the baggy, travel-stained trousers of her thermalsuit. With a childlike pout of displeasure she regarded the ungainly garments. And before either Nordgren or M'Cord could think or move to stop her, she opened the pressure-seams and stripped them off, letting them fall carelessly to her feet.

Nude and pure and lovely as an image of glowing alabaster, she stood poised before them for a moment—slim and cool and virginal, like a statuette of Diana or Psyche!

Then she threw back her head and laughed—a sweet, bell-like peal of happy laughter—innocent and carefree as a sprite.

And then she was gone.

They plunged after her, through the swinging tent-flap, out into the enshadowed garden, where luminous globules of uncanny opalescence floated on the breeze like goblin lanterns.

Like a fleeing dryad they glimpsed her white form go glimmering through the gloom of the garden and into the dark woods beyond.

And she was gone into the woods—naked and innocent and free, to join the golden and undying children who dwelt there.

"*Inga! INGA!*" Nordgren bawled out in a hoarse shriek. Intuitively guessing what he was about to do, M'Cord turned to hold him back—why, he did not know. But the other man twisted free and ran after the fleeing girl. He tripped and fell and stumbled through the flowers, and vanished in the direction the girl had gone.

And M'Cord stood there, baffled and helpless, wondering if the unseen guardians of Ophar were already beginning to strike them down invisibly, one by one. . . .

XXIII. By the Pool

Someone stood beside him, clutching his shoulder in strong fingers as if to restrain him from going after the two.

He turned with a growl to strike out; but it was Thaklar.

"What has happened here, my brother?" the Hawk prince demanded harshly.

"The Earth girl . . . touched by a bubble from the Pool . . . she ran naked into the woods. . . ."

"And her brother?"

"Nordgren went after her to bring her back."

Thaklar nodded grimly, his eyes brooding and thoughtful.

"So it has begun, at last," he said somberly. M'Cord made a move as if to pull away but the grip of those steely fingers tightened, restraining him.

"Do not go after them, my brother. Stay out of it."

"But—Inga—!" protested M'Cord.

"You have chosen her for your woman, have you not? Well, do not fear. If she has been touched but lightly— only one bubble, did you not say?—then she may recover knowledge of herself soon; and she will be safer in the woods than here, where the emanations of the Pool are more numerous and more frequent."

"But we can't just let her go off by herself like this, damn it!" M'Cord swore.

Thaklar shook his head gently. "Among the children of the woods she will be safe. There is nothing to harm her there, where even the beasts do not kill to feed . . ."

Suddenly remembering the lithe cat-creature he had watched at the edge of the Valley, and how it had fed on a ripe fallen fruit, M'Cord realized that there was something in Thaklar's words, after all. The Hawk prince had been of a lineage which from the beginning of time had guarded some of the secrets of Ophar; perhaps he knew more about the enchanted Valley and its mysteries than he had told.

"What about Nordgren? He ran off to find her, to bring her back . . ."

"He will never return. The Change is upon him, as well, I fancy. It is thus that the Valley defends its own . . . Have you hurt yourself, my brother? Your hand—"

M'Cord looked down to realize for the first time that his knuckles were cut and bleeding.

He shrugged. "I struck him—pulled them apart," he grunted. In a few, short words he described the scene he had interrupted, and what Inga and Nordgren had been engaged in before he had come bursting in upon them.

An expression of fastidious distaste flickered in Thaklar's fierce yellow eyes. But a shadow of pity was there, as well.

"A sickness, this thing between brother and sister . . . I have heard of such sicknesses before, but they are rarely found among my people."

"Thank God, they're rare enough among my people too, I'm glad to say!" The other man smiled softly.

"But are the same sort of things happening to the others?" he asked Thaklar. The warrior replied that he did

188

not know. M'Cord scratched the stubble on his jaw. "I left Phuun over that away, dead drunk," he began. Light flashed up in Thaklar's eyes.

"Did you tell him about the Pool?" the prince demanded with a strange urgency throbbing in his voice which M'Cord could not understand. Bewilderedly, M'Cord nodded and started to describe the revelation he had learned from the inebriated priest, but Thaklar cut him off with a sharp gesture.

"Come—swiftly! It matters not what they had planned; the Valley is awake now. Forces have been set in motion by our own deeds that could destroy us all. Come—which way *is* the Pool?"

M'Cord told him as best he could. Thaklar headed in that direction, running. Not understanding any of this, M'Cord began racing to keep up with the flying strides of the other.

The garden was dark and desolate and curiously deserted. Suddenly M'Cord realized what was so strange about its appearance, and that was that the Ushongti had vanished. Usually there were three or four of the amiable, fat lizard-folk to be seen waddling here and there about the pond or the flowerbeds at any given hour of the night or the day.

Now, not a single one was anywhere to be seen!

It was odd; it was strange. Where could they have gone? Where could they all be hiding—and *why?*

They found Phuun where they had expected to find him. He was kneeling by the brink of the Pool, at its very lip. And in his hands was the ceramic wine bottle he had been drinking from when M'Cord had last seen him.

Now the bottle was empty; soon it would be full again —but not with wine!

"We must stop him!" M'Cord said, trying to pass Thaklar; but the Hawk prince restrained him.

"Why?" he asked simply. "He has reached at last that for which he came so far to find. It would be unwise to come between him and that which he sought. Let him bring down upon him his own doom, as do all who come here with evil in their heart. And, besides, my brother: are we entirely free of guilt in this matter, you and I? Had it not been for my aid, they could never have come through the Broken Land. And you—what have you done?"

It occurred to M'Cord, as he stood there, that he must somehow have revealed to the drunken priest the spot where the Pool could be found. He could not recall having said it in so many words, but with an unconscious nod or glance he must have shown the renegade priest the true direction.

He bit his lip and fell silent. Side by side, they stood watching the sacrilege.

He was very drunk by now, was Phuun. So drunk that he could no longer stand erect. He must have crawled on his hands and knees up the three shallow crystal steps, and between the spiral-fluted pilasters to the edge of the Pool that lay beneath the dome that was like an immense crystal lens, focusing unknown rays from the depths of the void to play eternally upon the seething foam of the Water of Life.

He crouched there, giggling and tittering to himself, fondling with claw-like hands the empty bottle.

His eyes saw nothing but the Pool, and the Glory it contained. The brilliance of the luminous fluid bedazzled him; he stared, half blinded, into the curdled and seething radiance, a beatific smile upon his wrinkled face.

Then, muttering and crooning to himself—in words too faint for them to hear—he bent and plunged both hands in the blazing foam!

He straightened up, the bottle filled with liquid light, blazing like a lamp of hollowed agate in his hands. With

190

wet, trembling hands, which glowed faintly from the luminosity, he raised the bottle to his lips—

But did not drink thereof.

For the bubbles claimed him for their own.

He had stirred and roiled the waters of the Pool when he plunged his arms therein. Now the foam frothed and bubbled, disturbed by his touch. And from the fragile foam lifted a wobbling cluster of opal globules that floated about him like a storm of soap-bubbles.

They touched him everywhere—upon the brow, the eyes, the face, the hands. They touched his robe in a hundred places. And, with each touch, they vanished . . . it was as if his dry and thirsty body drank them in.

But not merely one bubble, as had sunk into the soft vale between Inga's breasts, erasing the lines of care from her features and the stain of guilt from her eyes, making her young and joyous and innocent again—but bubbles in their dozens and their hundreds that rose and clustered about the unwary priest, and vanished into him. . . .

What followed was uncanny.

Suddenly the aged priest was gone.

His robes fell in upon themselves, collapsing upon emptiness.

The ceramic bottle fell to the crystal pave and broke in a thousand ringing shards.

A loose bundle of robes lay there in a heap. But the gaunt and mummy-like figure of Phuun . . . was gone!

Then there came waddling through the twilight a comical, fat-paunched, scarlet lizard with great, solemn, humorous, and philosophical eyes under its trilobate crest of gold.

It was the Ushongti they called Old One.

It waddled and flopped up the steps and under the crystal dome. Squatting on its hind legs, its stubby tail thrust out behind to balance it in a position absurdly like that of a kangaroo, the Old One folded its four-fingered paws over its fat belly and peered down solemnly and at the soiled, bedraggled bundle of discarded raiment. Then it bent to poke about in the tangle of cloth.

It drew therefrom a naked infant.

It was small and rosy-golden; and it kicked fat legs sleepily, and cooed and gurgled. Like some ridiculous caricature of a nurse, the fat, wise old lizard cuddled the tiny naked thing against its wobbling paunch—cradled it gently in unhuman, scarlet-scaled arms. With one pointed, gold claw-tip it tickled the babe and made it laugh!

Then, as M'Cord watched with dazed, bewildered, unbelieving eyes, the Old One turned and waddled off, the baby cradled tenderly against its scaly breast. It vanished in the gloom that had come down upon the garden . . . and was gone!

"What—?" M'Cord mumbled between stiff lips.

"The mysteries of Ophar are beyond our knowledge and beyond the reach of our comprehension," Thaklar said.

"But what will happen to—to—?"

The princeling shrugged.

"The Ushongti will care for the babe, as they have done before, until such time as it is grown enough to join the naked children in the woods," he said. "Come . . . let us go. We can do nothing here, now; there will be no defilement of this place."

He turned and strode back in the direction of the camp.

M'Cord took a last look at the Pool, then followed him.

As for Phuun, the Valley had been kind. He had been given that which he had come here in search of. More of youthfulness than he might have wished, but then, that is often the way with those who seek miracles. Sometimes they find them to be greater than they had desired, and more irrevocable.

Phuun had found peace. He had even found judgment —of a sort.

XXIV. The Walking Trees

M'Cord went stumbling back to camp at Thaklar's heels in a numb, wordless daze.

The pearly twilight had deepened now into velvet gloom. Above them, the under-surface of the illusory barrier that was the "sky" of the enchanted Valley was a dome of darkest jade. Still from rim to rim the ripples of gilt light wandered. The sky was like a calm lake inverted above them by some sorcerer's spell, its placid waters trembling with the light of unseen stars.

They had come here to rape Eden, to despoil it of its treasures. But those treasures were calm, and peace, and innocence, and eternal youthfulness.

This was an Eden with no Serpent in it. They had each brought into Eden their own Serpent, coiled within their breasts, gnawing and feeding upon their own hearts.

For Inga the Valley had brought release from shame and guilt, escape from intolerable memories, and freedom.

For Karl the Valley had brought madness, or so it seemed: for he had run off bellowing into the night like a maddened thing.

For Phuun the Valley had brought erasure of his sins—retrogression into the innocence of infancy. He would grow into a young boy again with time, but he would become a different person. Phuun, or that collection of experiences and memories and traits grouped together under that name, was no more.

To him the Valley had been kind. It had given him that which is but rarely given to mortal man . . . a second chance!

And—the others? What had become of them under the pall of darkness which so mysteriously enshrouded the garden?

They found Zerild near the camp. The dancing girl was wild-eyed and distraught. She hurried to them as if eager for the reassurance of their normalcy.

"Has the world gone mad?" she blurted. Her face was flushed, her silken hair disordered, and fear was naked in her immense eyes. "Chastar became drunk with the golden wine and sought to force himself upon me," she gasped. "I fought him off and fled into the woods to escape him. There I beheld the *F'yagha* girl, naked as a child, laughing with the golden children and gathering flowers. She did not seem to know me nor to understand my words!"

Thaklar nodded somberly. "The girl was touched by one of the shining bubbles, and her mind has been washed clean of all memories. We go in search of her now."

"There is yet more!" Zerild panted. "Her brother! I met him, blundering and crashing through the brush, roaring like a maddened *slidar*. His face was streaming blood, and his clothes were ripped away. He did not seem to know me, either. He . . . he went on all fours, like a beast! Has the whole world gone mad, or is it I?"

Thaklar grunted, his face moody, yet there was fierce satisfaction in his eyes.

"The Valley defends itself by strange magic against intruders," he said. "Those who are free of evil taint, forced against their will to enter here, may escape enchantment. All others are—*changed*. But what of the wolf? You saw him not after fleeing from him? He did not follow you into the further woods?"

The frightened girl shook her head, eyes wide, and opened her mouth to speak. But at that moment a shrill cry rang out—the voice of a young girl, lifted in fear and pain.

"*Chastar!*" the Hawk prince swore.

"That sounded like one of the children," said M'Cord. Thaklar seized his arm with fingers like steel clamps. Suddenly there was fear in his eyes, too.

"If he has dared to lay hands of lust upon one of them . . ." he muttered. He did not finish the remark, but left the words hanging in the air.

"What, then?" demanded the Earthman.

Thaklar shook his head ominously. "Then must we all fear for our lives, my brother! For if the Sleeping Ones awaken—"

"You mean the gods?"

"No; those that were left here by the gods to protect the sanctity of the Valley. The lizard-folk but tend the gardens and the Pool; *but there are others. . . .*"

Zerild clutched his shoulder, nodding to the circle of trees which ringed the garden.

"The cry sounded as if it came from there," she said. With a curt word to M'Cord, Thaklar began to run in the direction from which the scream had come. He had bidden M'Cord stay behind, but the Earthman ignored it. If there was danger of some sort, he refused to linger behind while Thaklar faced it alone.

195

He had noticed that peculiar circle of trees when first they had come into this enchanted place. They had been spaced with such regularity as to suggest that they had been planted by intelligent direction. And they had completely encircled the garden, like a protective wall. M'Cord had puzzled over it at the time, but so many strange discoveries and marvels had come to his attention since that he had let this little strangeness slip his mind. But he remembered they were oddly different from the other trees that grew in the forests further down the Valley.

They found Chastar by the trees.

He had seized upon one of the golden children. Sometimes they wandered idly into the gardens, for no particular reason. M'Cord had seen them dancing on the mossy turf, or splashing in the lake, or playing amidst the flowers. They paid scant attention to the six outsiders, did not answer their questions, and soon wandered off again into the dim, far places.

But this young girl had wandered in alone, and had chanced to be found by the drunken outlaw, who was inflamed and frenzied by the wine the lizard-folk brewed.

He had seized her and pulled her down and was struggling with her on the turf when Thaklar burst upon the scene, with M'Cord not far behind.

The girl was adolescent; perhaps she did not understand what Chastar was trying to do, but the violence and hunger of him frightened her, and she had cried out. Now he was fighting to master her, his hands moving over her tender young body, his mouth seeking hers fiercely. The bewildered innocent fought like a young tigress but she was only a child and Chastar was a fully grown man, and a powerful one.

Thaklar bore no weapons, of course; nor did M'Cord. And the outlaw wore his energy guns strapped to his thighs. But there was no need for them to attempt to subdue him with their bare hands.

For one of the guardians was . . . *awake!*

The girl struggled in Chastar's arms and again she cried out—a single, piercing, bell-like note.

Behind them one of the trees . . . *stirred.*

Its roots pulled up out of the soil with a sucking sound. Its drooping, willow-like branches, which quivered to a wind that none of them could feel, now coiled and trembled with tension as the upper body of a cobra vibrates before it strikes.

M'Cord did not need Thaklar's arm to restrain him from going forward. He stood as if rooted to the spot, and his blood turned to ice within his veins as he watched the incredible thing.

The tree had pulled itself up out of the soil by now. It sidled forward, hairy black roots wriggling beneath it like snakes. Drooping fronds bent forward extended toward the outlaw, who saw or knew nothing but the slim childlike body that lay helpless, panting in the circle of his arms.

Then the tree was upon him. Branches flashed like slithering tentacles to encircle his throat. His eyes bulged in an expression of shocked amazement that would have seemed comical at another time. His mouth opened to yell —to curse—but no sound came therefrom.

Branches lashed about him like the coils of an anaconda. They pulled him off the girl and dangled him in the air, inches above the mossy turf, kicking and struggling frantically.

The sobbing girl sprang to her feet and darted off with a single frightened backward glance.

"We must help him," M'Cord growled between his teeth. Thaklar shook his head.

"We can do nothing to help him now," he said heavily. "And if we try, the other Sleeping Ones will rouse themselves to deal with us in the same manner. They sleep but lightly, you see. . . ."

He turned; Zerild was there watching, cramming her knuckles into her open mouth so that she would not scream. He put his arms about her shoulders and turned her about so that she could not see the end of it.

"Come," he said. They went back into the garden while the tree crushed the life from Chastar the red wolf.

XXV. When the Valley Woke

No longer did the Valley seem fair and tranquil. There were forces within it, they now knew, that were vast and hidden and terrible. Forces that could transform an old, old man into a puling infant, or drive a girl over the brink of madness, or slay a man suddenly and horribly.

On the way back, Zerild fell to her knees and was sick— rackingly, horribly sick. It was as if she spewed up all the venom and rancor that had built up within her all these years of treachery and betrayal.

It left her pale and weak and shaken. But Thaklar tended her gently, as one might tend a child. He wiped the vomit from her face with a bit of cloth, hushed her tears, and when she was too weak to stand, he gathered her up in his strong arms and bore her thusly back to their camp, her head swaying with exhaustion, drooping wearily against his chest.

By the margin of the pond he put her down and gave her cool water to drink.

Then he squatted beside her on his heels, staring off into the gloom that hung over the garden.

The Ushongti were not to be seen. The lizard-folk were

gone from the garden, to whatever place they nested. Nor were any more of the naked children of the woods to be found amidst the gardens.

Only the three of them were left.

"I should have seen it coming," Thaklar muttered heavily. "The darkness. It is the Night-of-Gods, the *khiah-i-huatha* whispered of in the oldest myths. The Darkening-time. It comes over the Valley when the sleeping forces stir and wake to protect The Holy against those who would intrude upon and defile its tranquility."

"Can we get out alive, do you think?" M'Cord asked hoarsely.

"If we leave now, perhaps. But we must be gone at once, and without delay."

M'Cord started to move, then paused.

"What about Inga? And Nordgren. We can't just *leave* them here!"

Thaklar was sweating; it glistened on his brow and on the bridge of his nose. He shook his head.

"Listen to me, 'Gort, my brother. This Valley is like a great machine, designed for a purpose. For many purposes. The gods are not here: they sleep in Yhoom—wherever and whatever Yhoom may be, which I know not. But it is not a machine of metal parts, such as those your people brought here. The Valley machine is composed of forces, forces vast and huge and powerful beyond our comprehension. Forces balanced against each other in tension, and bound together in rhythm and equipoise. We have disturbed that delicate balance by merely coming here; we disturb it, even now, simply by being here. Like a great machine, the Valley has resources built into its very nature for cleansing itself of impurities. Of grit, you could say. Once those forces have been stirred to wakefulness, they are swift to slay—as the red wolf was slain when he sought to violate the child. Nothing that creates a disturbance within the interplay of those forces whereof the machine is composed is permitted to exist here for very long. If we leave here now, taking nothing with us that is of the Valley, we may yet escape with our lives, and with ourselves unchanged, save in those matters wherein already the Valley has changed us. But to linger once the Darkening-time has come is madness and folly. We must go now, or remain here forever, and be changed—to innocent, forgetful childishness, as was the *F'yagha* girl, or to brutish madness, as I suspect the *dok-i-tor* her brother has been changed."

It was an impassioned speech, a display of volubility unusual for Thaklar, who was of nature a man of few words. But M'Cord refused to be swayed by them.

"I'm not going without the girl," he said stubbornly. "And that's that. Maybe you're right, and we should get out of here now before we get killed by those walking trees . . . but I don't know, Thaklar; I don't set such a big value on myself, that I can hightail it out of here and leave Inga behind to take care of herself . . ."

"She has forgotten you; she has even forgotten herself," said Thaklar somberly. "The Valley has taken her into itself by now, I think. What is the word you Outworlders use? *Assimilated;* the Valley has assimilated her. She is a part of it."

"Maybe. And maybe not. She was only touched by one bubble, remember. Anyway, whether she's lost her memories permanently or not, she deserves a chance. My people have remedies for the mind that has been injured or made ill; I owe her that much, at least. To see her taken care of. Whether she ever remembers me or not."

Thaklar looked at him with a wondering and bemused expression on his face. And when he laughed, softly, it was a laughter that had no bitterness nor mockery in it.

"The Valley has changed you, too, my brother: whether you know it yet or not."

"Eh?"

"I think that you have learned how to love a woman again," Thaklar said gently. "When you came here, there was a wound deep within you. You had been hurt sorely once, by a woman—as had I. There was a hard thing within you, a core of bitterness, like a knot of scar-tissue—a scab upon the heart. And now the Valley has worked its magic upon you, healing that wound as the Old One healed your torn leg, making it sound and whole again. Do you not love the woman, my brother?"

"I—" M'Cord started to speak, then checked himself and hesitated. What, after all, had passed between them except a few unimportant words, and a single kiss?

"I think you're right; I do love her; God help me!" he said at last, in a choked voice.

Thaklar smiled gently.

"God will help you, I think. The Valley understands love, my brother. It is the twin of happiness, and the brother of peace. Love is one of the forces that go to make up the wholeness of the machine. Very well, then; we will search for her together, you and I. Perhaps the guardians of the Valley will know and understand—for they sleep no longer, since we have awakened them in our folly and madness!"

M'Cord was vastly relieved. He said as much, gruffly, as was his way. Thaklar nodded.

"But there is one thing which we must do, 'Gort my brother. We must leave this place, and make our new camp at the edge of the Valley where the steps are cut into the stone of the cliff-wall. From that place we can search the woods for your woman . . . it will be a sign to the forces which, even now, watch us that our intentions are to leave here as soon as possible. . . ."

He got to his feet purposefully.

But he did not walk away.

For suddenly Zerild was there. She had thrown herself

202

at his feet, sobbing wildly. And her arms crept up to embrace his long legs. And he looked down at her with an expression written upon his face in a language of the heart which even M'Cord could read.

XXVI. *The Surrender*

She lifted her face to him. It was wet with tears and wild with conflicting emotions. And her eyes—no longer sharp and fierce with mockery—were frightened and open as those of a child.

"Do not leave me. Take me with you," she panted.

"Now why should you, who spurned me once, wish to go at my side now?" he asked quietly.

She shook her head furiously, black tresses tousling over slim, bare shoulders. And she clung to his legs with surprising strength.

"I cannot ask you to forgive me, prince. And I do not ask it. Take me with you on any terms you like. As your woman! Or your servant. Even as your slave. But do not leave me alone here in this awful place where men are turned to babes or beasts, or rent apart by trees that have learnt to walk! I will cook for you, tend your beasts, mend your clothes. Anything! I will do anything you ask—only do not leave me alone in this place where trees can walk and women go mad! Take me with you, I beg of you—yes, I—even I!—Zerild!—who never begged aught of a man before—beg it of you, of you whom I have wronged so terribly—and laughed at—and made mockery of—and spurned! See me, prince! Tamed and humbled at last . . . and do not spurn me, prince, as once I wantonly did spurn you. . . ."

He bent and grasped her shoulders and drew her to her feet.

"Well," he said gruffly. "Well, perhaps I shall take you along to make the meals. But do not grovel at my feet like a whipped *khirth!* When you were proud and free and untamed, I loved you. I do not love servility; but you can come—to mend my raiment and prepare my meals, remember! Only that, nothing more!"

Despite the harshness of his words, his voice was tender and almost joking, and there was something in his face which M'Cord had never seen there before, nor ever thought to see.

She saw it, too, the woman. And smiled through her tears and the tangle of her long black hair—a smile no longer proud or mocking, but shy, curiously shy—as a young girl smiles when for the first time she has seen ardor and the desire for her in the face of a boy.

And he smiled, too; and something was decided between them, and M'Cord guessed—correctly—that, whatever would be there between them in the days to come, it would not be a matter of the mending of clothing or the making of meals.

He watched them with wonderment, and shook his head.

The Valley had worked its magic upon the two of them, as well. On Thaklar. On Zerild!

They, too, were changed.

They, too, were—healed! And whole again.

Without even taking the time to eat the evening meal, they bundled up their gear and made ready to depart. Thaklar cautioned them against taking along anything that was part of the Valley. They could not even fill the waterskins from the pond.

The gear that had belonged to the others they simply left where it lay. But Thaklar took the weapons Chastar had stripped from them back in Ygnarh, and the outlaw's weapons as well, save for the pistols he had worn when the walking tree had slain him.

The other gear they left behind. The extra blankets and bedrolls and clothing. There was no point in loading themselves up with things they would not need and could not easily carry. And, said Thaklar, the garden could—cleanse itself. That which they discarded would quickly crumble into dust, he said. For decay is one of the forces built into the world-old machine that was the Valley; thus it was that it rid itself of that which did not belong here.

And there was something to his words, M'Cord realized with a shiver. The tent Nordgren had put up still stood, a blot on the tranquility of the eternal garden. But the tent was not eternal, and already the insidious forces of decay were at work upon it. The heavy nioflex of which it was made was tough and sturdy—durable enough to hold its sheen through a decade of use. But already it was dull and blotchy-looking; a film of mold had rooted itself in the glistening synthetic fabric, and had eaten into the material, fretting its edges into raggedness. And something had gotten into the vacuum pockets of the flap, opening the pressure-seams that should have been able to withstand hurricanes without parting. Now the flaps dangled open, loosely swaying in the breeze.

The tent already had the look of something abandoned —dilapidated—slumping into decay.

M'Cord was glad to be gone from this uncanny place where the sturdiest synthetic fabric in existence crumbled to rags overnight. And he was fretful and impatient, nervous at each moment of delay.

That feeling of being watched by unseen eyes was upon him again. He felt eyes against his back, and the sensation was so uncanny that it made his skin creep and his nape-hairs stiffen like a dog's hackles.

They all felt it; Zerild was subdued and obedient, and her eyes clung constantly to Thaklar, as if for reassurance —as if she drew strength and comfort from his very nearness. She did not leave his side for a moment, if she could help it.

It would have been nice to have made their goodbyes to the Old One and his friendly, hospitable brethren, but the Ushongti were nowhere to be seen and must still be hidden in their nests, whose whereabouts none of them had ever known. With a little pang of guilt, M'Cord realized that he had never even thanked the great, comical, kindly lizard-creature for the healing of his crippled leg. So suddenly had events rushed forward to their climax, and so bewildering had been the discoveries and transformations of this single day, that it had slipped his mind.

But perhaps it didn't matter. Perhaps the wise, philosophical old lizard could read the gratefulness in his heart with its strange, telepathic gifts. He hoped so.

He stood for a moment, making a silent goodbye to the garden and to those who tended it, remembering all that had happened to him here.

Then he turned, shouldered his knapsacks, and trudged after Thaklar and Zerild, in the direction of the edge of the Valley.

M'Cord had half expected that when they reached the wall of the walking trees they would find the sleeping guardians awake, aroused, and alert to stand against them.

But this did not happen. The trees were awake, all right, their tentacular branches stirring with unnatural agitation, but they remained firmly rooted in the sod. The three travelers passed swiftly through the ring of their boles—shudderingly aware of being watched by truculent, suspicious, even hostile eyes—but emerged therefrom onto the mossy plains without being attacked or even having their way impeded.

The mysterious darkness still cloaked the Valley. They could not see across its breadth to the far walls of the crater. But Thaklar led them to the foot of the stony stair with that unerring compass-like faculty the Martians have, and nothing happened to disturb or alarm them along the way.

They entered the woods cautiously, for here it was very dark indeed, and there was no telling what might be lurking within the gloom, awaiting them.

The naked children had fled, it seemed, into the deepest parts of the forest. At least they encountered not a one of the slim, golden inhabitants of the wood during their journey through it.

In one moonless glade, however, they encountered a beast.

It was one of the primordial cat-creatures, such as M'Cord had seen upon first entering the Valley. Then it had eyed him indifferently, paying no attention to his presence. Now the lithe, tawny thing that Nordgren had suggested might be a living fossil from the past—an ancestor of the Martian race; one of the beasts from whose flesh the Timeless Ones had shaped and molded the Firstborn of the People in the Beginning—now it turned upon them, the great cat, baring long ivory fangs in a snarl of menace, eyes burning green-gold through the velvet gloom.

It made no move to attack them, however; it crouched at the far end of the glade, growling deep in its chest in an attitude of watchful menace.

"It is even as I said," grunted Thaklar. "The Valley has turned against us now, and thrusts us forth from within it.

Even the placid, gentle beasts have turned against us and threaten us."

M'Cord nodded. Adam and Eve had been driven from their own garden thusly, by an angel with a flaming sword. And the eyes of that angel had blazed, he suspected, with watchful fires no less threatening than the eyes of the beast that crouched, spitting and growling, to watch them go.

And so they went from Eden.

XXVII. Expelled from Eden

Not long thereafter they emerged from the edge of the woods and found that Thaklar's sense of direction had proved unerring, for they were near the eastern wall of the immense crater, and the foot of the stone stair was before them.

They made camp there, in the open space between the bottom of the cliff and the margin of the forest. Bedrolls were laid out and a hasty, ill-prepared meal was devoured. They were too hungry and tense and fatigued to do more than wolf down the cold food, moisten their throats with water from the scant supplies in the waterskins, and turn to their blankets. It had been an endless day, thronged with strange discoveries and horrible events, and their minds were exhausted with marvels and revelations. They sank into a deep, dreamless sleep the moment they stretched out and composed themselves for slumber.

And dawn came, paling the inverted lake of sky, and they awoke, rested and refreshed. And the Night-of-Gods was over, they realized. No more did they endure the scrutiny of invisible eyes; no more did malignant life and sentience stir in the weird trees.

But they had been thrust out of Eden, and they knew it. They could not linger too long—even here, at the edge of the Valley—with impunity.

M'Cord was up before the others. He made his morning coffee and drank it down, draining it in savage gulps, hot, black, bitter, and strong. It drove the fogs of sleep from his brain, and filled him with a fixed sense of purpose, and a grim, unwavering determination to search the woods for some sign of Inga before starting the long road back to Ygnarh.

Thaklar volunteered to assist him, and Zerild would have come as well, had not the Hawk prince sternly bade her remain behind to tend the camp, to which she acquiesced with a meekness M'Cord had never before discerned in her demeanor.

It would seem that when Zerild surrendered herself to a man, she did so utterly! At last the dancing girl had found the man of all men who could master her! He grinned at Thaklar without words and the prince returned the smile, sensing M'Cord's thought.

He was vastly satisfied, was Thaklar. He had found that for which he had searched so long.

The Valley had given unto him according to his deserving.

They entered the woods and began to hunt for the missing girl. Even now, in the pearly twilight of dawn, the woods were empty. Not merely deserted; it was as if they had been abandoned by all life. The small creeping things who made of the forest their home had fled, or so it seemed, into the deep heart of the woods as if to avoid the taint of their presence. Naught rustled through the fallen leaves, or chittered from the motionless boughs, or scurried down the mossy aisles between the mighty boles of black and gnarled and knotted wood. Nor did they feel

212

the pressure of invisible eyes watching them as they searched.

And, toward midday, they found a glade deep within the forest, where a bubbling pool lay open beneath the jade-and-golden sky.

And the girl was there!

She lay nude, curled up on a cushion of sapphire moss, her golden hair spread about her. She was sleeping as a child sleeps, deeply and profoundly. And if she dreamed any dreams, they were peaceful and pleasant ones, for she smiled slightly in her slumber.

M'Cord bent over her and spoke her name hoarsely. She stirred in her sleep, and blinked up at him, blue eyes open and soft. The stain of guilt was gone from those eyes, he saw, and the shadow of shame. And her face no longer reflected the tension that had lined it with weariness: it was as calm and smooth and radiant as a young girl's. Whether the drifting bubble blown to her from the Pool of Life had taken years from her or merely cleansed her mind of all memories of sin, she looked years younger.

She smiled up at him sleepily, then yawned and stretched languidly and sat up.

"Oh, M'Cord! I have had the strangest dream," she said.

"You—remember me?" he demanded harshly.

Her eyelashes fell demurely, veiling the candor of her eyes.

"Of course I remember you," she said softly. "How could I forget—you!"

"Thank God!" he said in a voice that shook, and drew her to her feet. She came into the shelter of his arms as if coming home, to a place where she belonged. He crushed her to him, but tenderly, and their lips met. She returned the pressure of his mouth with a kiss that was at once virginal and passionate.

Then, over his shoulder, she caught sight of Thaklar as he stood there watching them with a small, gentle smile softening the hard planes of his face.

"Oh!" she murmured, breaking free of the embrace. And then, for the first time realizing her nakedness, she pinked in confusion. The rosy flush colored her face and neck and bosom, M'Cord saw. She attempted to cover herself with her hands and her hair.

But he had envisioned the possibility of finding her and had brought clothing from her gear. So while he and the Hawk prince retired from the glade, she slipped into the garments and rejoined them a moment or two later, flushed and breathless but in a fit condition for company.

They headed back to camp. She seemed to have taken no hurt or harm from her experiences and, when M'Cord cautiously asked her what she remembered of the events of yesterday, she seemed to find it difficult to remember much of anything.

"I don't know," she murmured hesitantly. "It all seems as though it had happened such a long time ago. . . . I remember the friendly Ushongti tending their flower-beds by the pond . . . and how you and I discovered the Pool of Life and . . . and . . . each other!" She dropped her eyes bashfully, but could not restrain her lips from smiling at the memory. "But . . . after that . . . I don't seem to remember very much. There was a fight or an argument, I forget which. . . ."

"And then? What happened then?" he prodded, anxious to discover the extent of her amnesia, if that's what it was.

She shook her head bewildered. Then she smiled—a calm, sweet smile of quickening joyousness that was like a sunrise in its serenity and promise.

"And then I went to play with the children in the woods," she said simply. "We had such happy games! And

214

then I got sleepy and . . . just went to sleep. And then you found me," she finished.

M'Cord did not try to awaken further memories, fearing to stir up things she would be happier to leave forgotten. She remembered her brother but seemed oddly incurious as to what had become of him. And she accepted without surprise that Phuun and Chastar would trouble them no more. She did not even seem to find it odd that Zerild was so changed, and when they re-entered their temporary camp at the foot of the cliffs, she exchanged calm greetings with the dancing girl in a friendly manner, seemingly indifferent to what had chanced to work so miraculous a transformation in the Martian woman.

It was as if the erasure of her memories had caused a mental trauma so violent and dramatic as to erect a wall between yesterday and today. A wall through which only happy memories could pass unhindered; a wall that made everything which had occurred in her former life dim and vague, remote and somehow not very important.

She seemed to have the greatest difficulty in remembering anything about her brother, Karl. Nor did it seem to bother her that he was no longer with them. It was as if he belonged to the past, and was among all the many things she had put behind her.

M'Cord guessed that her every memory of Karl Nordgren was so intrinsically bound up with pain and guilt and fear that when the bubble from the Pool had cleansed her of these taints it had wiped away most of her remembrances of him.

To her, too, the Valley had been kind.

It had given to Inga according to her deserving.

XXVIII. The End of It

But the Valley was not yet done with them, it seemed. There was one final revelation that awaited them before they could put Ophar, its beauties and marvels and terrors, behind them forever.

It lurked, waiting for them, half-hidden behind a flowering bush. Inga shrieked and hid her eyes from the hideousness of the thing that crouched there; Thaklar jerked out an oath and went for his gun. M'Cord laid a hand on his arm to halt him, for the thing did not attack, it crouched there snarling and spitting.

It was hunched and deformed and hideous, its twisted nakedness begrown with dirty tufts of yellow fur. Yellow shag hung across its features, which were twisted in a maniacal snarl of rage and menace. They could see long white fangs bared by the lifting of bearded lips, and the canine muzzle wrinkled, the nostrils open and distended. And through the tangled, matted mane of shaggy fur the eyes that blazed with blue fires were filled with madness.

Its arms ended in dirty paws and its loins and lower limbs were shaggy and satyr-like, terminating in hooves which stamped and tore the turf. It snarled and spat and gobbled at them in a horrible travesty of articulate speech, gesticulating in a threatening manner. But it did not charge them and they passed it hurriedly, with wary backward glances.

"I—I thought all the beasts had fled from this part of the woods!" M'Cord said, breathing easily once the grimacing satyr had vanished into the depths behind them and they were safely past it and into the open space.

"They have. That was no—beast. I will tell you later what I mean," Thaklar grunted enigmatically.

Inga uncovered her eyes and peered about.

"How—horrible! Is it gone?" she whispered timidly. "I —I didn't know there were such ugly things in the forest. . . ."

"It is gone, and will threaten us no more," Thaklar said with strange finality in his tones, and an odd satisfaction, too.

Then they greeted Zerild, and broke camp, and departed at last from the Valley.

And from behind its screen of bushes at the forest's edge, the thing that Karl Nordgren had become watched them go with burning eyes, and hated them.

It was a long climb to the top of the crater wall, but they made it without too much trouble. Something in the air of the Valley had filled them with energy. They felt, all of them, years younger and far more vital and vigorous. Their strength and endurance and their ability to resist fatigue seemed extraordinary, even to themselves.

Perhaps it was due to the Pool of Eternity. Perhaps some of its vital energies leaked into the very air of the Valley, charging all who breathed thereof with renewed vigor and stamina.

They did not know how else to explain it; but they were aware of the freshness and strength that welled up within them as they climbed. The task should have left them trembling with exhaustion, but it did not. And they reached the rim of the crater tired and aching, but not overly so.

The shock of emerging from the unnatural warmth and humidity of the oxygen-rich atmosphere of Ophar into the cold, dry air of Mars took its toll on all of them, however. Inga and Zerild had to rest, panting and shivering, while their bodies slowly adapted to the abrupt change. Even Thaklar found some difficulty in adjusting. They lay there, gasping for breath, pulses drumming, looking down into the crater. From this height the illusion was complete and the falsity of the mirage was thoroughly indetectable. They could have sworn the bottom of the crater was only a barren desert plain littered by crumbling boulders.

The Valley, it seemed, would protect its secret for ages more. . . .

At the foot of the crater wall they found tracks of the *slidars*. An hour's search of the winding maze that was the Broken Land and they had found two of the beasts. The others they never found.

Like the terrestrial camel, the Martian *slidar* can go a very long time without water. Unlike the camel, the loper can also endure a considerable period of time without food and still retain its strength.

Letting the two women ride, with the men leading the beasts, they began the long road back to Ygnarh. Their supplies of food were considerably depleted, but the pressure-still could keep their supplies of water intact for long periods, providing that they could find vegetation. It took lengthy side trips to find places in the deep crevices where the hardy and omnipresent rubbery-leafed moss grew in numbers plentiful enough to supply them with drinkables.

They were three days and nights on the Road back. They took the trip in easy stages, cautious of exhausting the beasts. But the *slidars* were hardier than they could have hoped and were still in pretty good condition when the ruins of Ygnarh hove into view.

For nearly a week they rested in Ygnarh, hunting game in order to replenish their supplies of food and storing up water in the waxed skins. The principal reason for the extended period of relaxation was to strengthen the *slidars* after their long ordeal.

Thaklar and M'Cord decided the wisest thing to do was to destroy the notes and files Nordgren had prepared. Let immemorial Ygnarh remain a legend for another million years, they agreed; and let the Valley remain a myth forever.

They did not consult Inga in this. She seemed to have almost completely forgotten about her brother, and it seemed wiser to let what few of her memories she retained sleep undisturbed.

And so they rested, the lovers, and contemplated the long journey that still lay ahead of them.

The week was over all too swiftly, it seemed. Soon enough it would be time to go. They rode a little way together, but before very long it was time to make the last farewells.

"Where will you and your woman go, Thaklar?"

The prince smiled. "We shall go back to the lands of my people," he said quietly. "Southward, across the Regio and along the edges of the dead sea bottom of the Noachis, by means of the Aurum Iani Fretum; this season my nation encamps in Argyre, far to the south. We will follow one of the canals—most likely Argyroporos—as far as we are able." He used, of course, the native names rather

220

than those invented by Earthside astronomers. But M'Cord knew well enough what he meant.

"I had not known any of the Nine Nations camped so near the southern pole," he said. "Anyway—will your people accept you back amongst them, do you think?"

Thaklar shrugged. "Only the gods know the answer to that question, my brother. But if they do not, then we shall dwell apart, Zerild and I. Perhaps in the native quarter of one of your *F'yagha* colonies; perhaps in Yeolarn itself, in the Old City. At least I will have done this much; I will be able to tell the princes of my clan that those who stole the secret are dead. And I will return into the keeping of my House that which was taken therefrom."

He touched the saddlebag where he had placed the worn and ancient disk of silver.

"It does not greatly matter to me now whether my exile ends," he said, smiling into the eyes of Zerild, who rode beside him. "For now I am no longer alone."

"Nor will you ever be, my lord," she whispered.

M'Cord grinned.

Thaklar returned the question.

"And you, 'Gort? Where will you and your woman go? Back to the *F'yagha* colony at Lacus Solis?"

"Yep. It's nearest. Back the way I came, I think; north through Aram and then down south again, keeping to the canals as best we can."

"And when you are there again—what then?"

He shrugged and grinned a trifle abashedly.

"Then I guess we'll find us a god-peddler, and get married!" Thaklar laughed affectionately.

"This, then, is our last meeting! Farewell to you and to your woman, O my brother, my friend! It is a long road we have gone together, you and I; and mayhap it does not end here . . . for, who knows? One day we shall meet again, if it be the will of the Timeless Ones. . . ."

M'Cord nodded wordlessly. He extended his hand. The

221

F'yagha gesture was not unknown to Thaklar; although it was not Custom, he took M'Cord's hand and wrung it in his own for a moment while they looked deep into each other's eyes without speaking, as men of their sort seldom do at such moments.

Then they parted. They wheeled their *slidars* about, exchanged one final salute, and rode off in opposite directions.

But only for a moment. Then Thaklar called out and M'Cord turned, tugging the head of his loper, bringing the beast to a halt in order to see what Thaklar wanted.

The Hawk princeling came jogging up to within two yards of where M'Cord sat in the saddle. He was grinning wolfishly.

"You have forgotten something, my brother!" he called.

"What?"

Thaklar drew back his arm and threw something.

"This!"

A small object flashed and sparkled through the air.

M'Cord caught it in his hand and looked down, opening his fingers. Purple radiance pulsed and flickered in his palm. He drew in his breath sharply. It was true: he *had* forgotten!

The purple ruby glowed and twinkled in the sunlight. It was the size of the ball of his thumb, and of the purest water. And the Martian *ziriol* was the rarest and most desirable of all precious stones.

He held a fortune cupped and blazing in his hand.

"Farewell once more, my brother!" called Thaklar. "Till we meet again!"

Then they separated and each began the long road home.